COMING HOME

FULLY INVESTED BOOK 1

KB ALAN

Copyright © 2020 by KB Alan

Edited by Kelli Collins
Cover by Word Sugar Designs

ISBN-13: 978-1-955124-00-3 (Paperback)
ISBN-13: 978-1-955124-03-4 (Large Print Paperback)
ISBN-13: 978-1-955124-06-5 (Hardback)
ISBN-13: 978-1-955124-09-6 (Large Print Hardback)

❀ Created with Vellum

DEDICATION

For Mom. Still, and every day.

Special thanks to Anita Williams and Kate Pearce xoxo

ABOUT THIS BOOK

Coming Home

Rose never expected to return to Wildlife Ridge after she graduated high school, but here she is, sixteen years later. She wants to spend some time focusing on her new life as an entrepreneur, away from the big city rat race, and her quiet hometown in the mountains seems like the perfect place to do that. She's excited to spend some time with her parents and has barely given a passing thought to seeing Ethan again. Really. Hardly at all.

Ethan hasn't seen Rose on her infrequent visits home. He's never forgiven himself for cancelling out on taking her to prom at the last minute. His life hasn't panned out the way he expected, but he loves his town, and he's hopeful she'll love it enough to stick around for awhile, give Wildlife Ridge a second chance. And maybe give him a chance to make it up to her after all this time.

To join KB Alan's newsletter, visit www.kbalan.com/newsletter

Rose watched her friend Naomi walk back to the car, swinging a grocery sack of snacks, and switching her hips from side to side. She grinned, glad her friend had taken the time to do this road trip with her. Leaving Southern California, where she'd been so happy the last several years, was going to be tough. Moving so far from her two best friends, Naomi and Janelle, was going to be tougher still.

The gas pump clicked and she took the nozzle out of the car as Naomi climbed inside. She twisted the gas cap into place and grabbed the receipt. This would be their last stop before they reached Wildlife Ridge, Colorado, population 2,235, last time she'd looked. The town she'd grown up in and never expected to return to.

"This is Bell View, the last big town before Wildlife Ridge. We've got about forty-five minutes to go," Rose told Naomi. "They reworked the highway and it's much better now. When I lived there it was a little over an hour to get here. This is where I'll come if I want to go to the movies or hit a Target."

Naomi looked around. "Forty-five minutes, huh? How many

Targets do you think we passed in the first forty-five minutes after we left Los Angeles?"

Rose laughed. "Probably ten. It's a different world out here in the mountains."

She flashed a grin at Naomi, who had queued up one of their favorite songs, which came blaring out of the radio as soon as Rose started the car. They hit the highway with the windows down, their voices high and her heart full. She would miss living in the same city as her friends, but they wouldn't lose their closeness. It had been obvious for a while that none of them were going to stay in Los Angeles long term, it just happened to turn out that Rose was the first to make the move.

When the song ended, Naomi turned the volume down a bit and checked the GPS. "Okay, so you have to go nearly an hour for a movie theater. Tell me there's a Starbucks in the actual town."

The horrified expression on her friend's face had Rose laughing. "Of course there is. And a McDonald's. An old-fashioned diner. A barbecue place. At least, last time I was there."

"Hmm. You know, I looked up the numbers. There are about the same number of people in this town as there were in my high school graduating class."

"Ha! My graduating class had fifty-four. If you count Donna Calender, who was held back to the next year."

"That's…I mean, I can't even…there's probably more people at my grocery store at any given time than there were in your whole senior class."

They busted up laughing, then turned the radio up for another favorite song. Naomi pulled a package of gummy worms out of her sack and handed a couple over.

"So, am I going to be the only person of color in this entire town for the duration of my visit?"

Rose threw her a sheepish look. "No, but it *is* like ninety-two percent white. Or, it was."

Naomi rolled her eyes. "I kind of already figured."

Chomping on a worm, Rose considered. "I realize I was probably an ignorant white kid, but I don't remember there ever being any racism in town. I mean, I'm sure there must have been, but definitely not systematic. My mom's best friend was—is—Black. And, okay, there was only one Black guy in my graduating class, but I was supposed to go to prom with him, and I never even thought twice about that."

Naomi flicked a worm in her direction. "Supposed to?"

"Well, the jerk canceled on me at the last second. He apologized, but I couldn't get past it and kind of ignored him until I left town." She glanced over. "But maybe he felt a little guilty, so that's why he was willing to give me the lease on this apartment as six months, instead of the usual twelve."

"Wait. You're telling me prom guy is the apartment manager you've been emailing with?"

"Yep. We never brought it up, our conversations have been strictly about negotiating and signing the lease, and sending me the keys, but he didn't fight me on changing the lease."

Naomi gave her a high-five. "You should still make him do a little groveling when you see him. I bet prom's an even bigger deal out here than it was for us."

"On the one hand, yes. But on the other hand, I was already planning my move to college in California and ready to leave this place, so it wasn't too big a deal. I really did like him though. Now that I look back, it was probably a good thing. I might have fallen head over heels and rethought my plans. He was going to college in Denver." She accepted the offered gummy worm, chewed. "Huh. I never really thought about it that way before. We had gotten friendly and he's a cool guy. I was so freaking excited when he asked me to prom." She shook her head. "Wow, what a difference sixteen years makes. I think it will be nice to see him."

"All right. So, we've got a Starbucks, a few restaurants, and at least two Black families in this town." Naomi stretched her legs out, reclined her seat back a little more. "But I still don't think this place is exactly in line with your plan to move somewhere with a low cost of living. Sure, it's lower than Los Angeles, but still about average for the country. Average is not low."

"That's why I only committed to six months. I figured it would be good to reconnect with my parents a bit and get used to small-town living again, without it being too rustic. Besides," she added, slapping her friend's leg, "you're the one who constantly reminds us that there's a difference between being frugal and being cheap."

"Fair enough."

Naomi offered another gummy worm, but Rose waved it off. Her friend had a super high metabolism that required a lot of calories. It had taken Rose and Janelle a little time to realize that Naomi was just as self-conscious about being too skinny as they were about the opposite. Janelle hovered on the side of plump, and used to make herself miserable with failed diets. She was better about it now, but still denied herself a lot. Rose was luckier. She wasn't thin by any means, and she'd probably need to start doing some actual exercise as she neared forty, but she'd reached a level of comfort with her body that neither of her girlfriends had managed.

She slowed down as they approached a logging truck. There were only two lanes on this stretch of highway, so she settled back to wait for a passing opportunity. Somehow, through sixteen years of living in LA, she'd managed to maintain her calm driving habits. Which made Naomi and Janelle nuts. They were especially disdainful of the fact that she always came to a full and complete stop at stop signs. Luckily, before Naomi had to bite through her lip to say anything, a passing lane appeared and she was able to zip past the truck.

Another favorite song came on, and she whooped as Naomi turned the volume back up. They danced in their seats, singing along at top volume, Naomi waving her hands in the air. The song had been a hit the year they'd been freshman at UCLA. She'd met her best friends there and been so happy. She never thought she'd be returning to sweet little Wildlife Ridge.

It wasn't that there was anything wrong with the town, other than it being so small and intimate. Everyone knowing your business, thinking they knew what was best for you all the time. But then again, they were actually there for you when you needed it. Mostly. And cared about what happened to you.

She'd never been more ashamed in her life than when she'd seen an ambulance at her apartment building, and realized she had no idea the name of her neighbor being wheeled out on a stretcher. She wouldn't have even recognized the man if she hadn't seen what unit he was coming from. There were certainly things she'd miss about Los Angeles, but that level of anonymity wasn't one of them.

They passed a highway sign letting them know they were fifteen miles from their destination.

"If you're really considering moving here, not just staying for a while, I want to know more," Naomi said. "Is it like, a mining town? Factory town? Tourists? How does everyone make their money?"

"First I want to concentrate more on surviving as an entrepreneur and worry about where I'll land later, but Wildlife Ridge is definitely in the running. It was a logging town way back when. Started by two brothers, with the last name of Rabbit. They didn't want to name the town after bunnies, so they went the more exotic route. And that somehow led to the fact that most of the streets and businesses in town are named after wildlife, so it ended up being kind of cutesy anyway."

Naomi snorted. "Nice."

"Logging has mostly died off in the area, though there's still a sawmill on the edge of town. It's not nearly as big an employer as it used to be, though. At some point Wildlife Ridge managed to become the county seat, even though there's the bigger town we left a while back. This was before my parents' time, but apparently there was drama. Maybe some fraud. That town got the small hospital, but Wildlife Ridge has the seat, whatever that really means. There's the sheriff's office, the Forest Service office and maintenance yard, that kind of stuff. There's a big state park nearby, so they get people who work there, as well as tourists who are camping there and want to come to town to eat and shop. Tourists stopping on their way to other cities or campgrounds. It's not a tourist town, per se, but there's always some around."

"Seems like a lot for a small town."

"Not when you're there," Rose laughed. "Let's see. There's the volunteer fire department, a Masonic Temple which rents their banquet hall out for all sorts of events, um...oh, the one funeral home is run by the guy who's also the county coroner."

"Of course he is."

"There's a ranch not far out of town. People stay there to go on long horseback camping rides in the mountains, or to train with horses, or have their horses trained. Or something like that. I don't really know, but it does mean we get cowboys in town sometimes. And wannabe cowboys."

"Could be interesting," Naomi said.

They'd gained a lot of elevation in the last hour and Rose had to clear her ears so they wouldn't pop. The mountains stretched up on either side of the highway, shades of green peeking out from blankets of snow. Since it was the middle of February, she hadn't much trusted the weather reports, but they'd had clear skies the whole trip. As they finally took the exit for the little town nestled in the mountains, she looked at it with fresh eyes.

The exit curved to the north, directly onto Main Street. Off to the right was the ever-present plume of steam from the sawmill. There were no stop signs going her direction, and no stop lights in town at all, just a caution light at Dragonfly road, where she turned to get to the apartment buildings she was going to call home. There were two more apartment buildings further down Main Street, sister buildings owned by the same company. They weren't really any nicer than Salmon Springs, but they were next to the park and lake, so they charged a bit more in rent, and Rose hadn't seen the point in that. The little town was nestled in a valley surrounded by forest and mountains, so she would be in the middle of the gorgeous views just by walking out the door, no need to pay a premium. She pulled into the lot and looked at Naomi.

"Welcome home," her friend said.

ETHAN PAUSED at the entrance to apartment 212. The door was wide open, likely for the cool blast of late-winter air. Music played, loudly but not too loudly, and the charming voice singing along had him pausing before he knocked on the doorjamb.

He'd wondered if he'd feel anything when he saw Rose again. High school was a lifetime ago, and he'd started to think some serious thoughts about her back in the day. But they'd been children, really. And he'd disappointed her, let her down. Story of his life. She'd grown up, he saw now. In all the right ways.

She did a little wiggle as she unwrapped some kind of figurine and placed it on the shelves in front of her, and he tried not to watch her ass. But he didn't try very hard. Even though her back was to him, he knew it was Rose. They'd known each other since kindergarten, after all. In a small town like Wildlife Ridge, it was impossible not to know someone your own age. They'd played together as children, but they'd never been especially close. Not until those last couple of months.

She was not sporting a California-girl tan, might even be paler than he remembered her. Apparently she hadn't turned into a beach bum during her life out in LA. Her previously long hair had been cut and shaped into a wavy brown mass that bounced on her shoulders and invited him to tug. He wanted her to turn around so he could see it framing her face.

Another voice joined hers in song, and he watched a long-legged Black woman dance her way down the hall to join Rose. They grabbed hands and circled around the room for a moment before Rose's eyes landed on him and she came to an abrupt halt.

He let his hand, knuckles still pointed towards the doorjamb, fall as she blinked at him from behind her glasses. That was another change. She'd almost always worn her contacts, once they got to junior high school.

"Hey," he said, sounding lame to his own ears. "Sorry to interrupt. I just wanted to bring you this, and make sure you have everything you need." He held up a spider plant. "Welcome to Salmon Springs apartment building."

She dusted her hands along her thighs and came to him, reaching for the plant. "Wow, that's so sweet, thanks. It's good to see you, Ethan."

"Rose. It's been a long time."

"This is one of my best friends, Naomi Washington. Naomi, Ethan Woodford."

The woman who approached him was all city. At least, that's what he chose to attribute the air of no-nonsense confidence to. He supposed she'd heard about him and was prepared to be unimpressed.

"Ma'am," he said, as he offered his hand.

She blinked at him, apparently astonished. Then she looked to Rose. "Did he just insult me to my face?"

Rose's lips twitched and she adjusted her glasses higher up her nose. "No. He was being sincerely polite."

Naomi stared at her friend for a moment, then returned her attention to him. "It's nice to meet you."

He shook her hand, forcing back a grin. Yeah, she was all city.

"Naomi's helping me move. She took a little vacation to drive out with me."

"How was the drive?" he asked, leaning back against the doorjamb.

"We broke it up into two days, but with the big push yesterday. Spent the night just inside Colorado. It wasn't too bad."

He nodded. "Be sure and let me know if I can help out with anything. I've got my toolbox, in case you haven't unpacked that yet." He nearly shook his head at how stupid that sounded. Her parents owned a hardware store, for crying out loud, surely she'd have access to whatever she needed.

She raised her eyebrows. "Thanks, will do."

He nodded, backed up. "You have my cell, just call or text if you need anything. It was nice to meet you, Naomi."

They said their goodbyes and he retreated, shaking his head in disgust at himself as he walked down the hallway. It wasn't like he didn't interact with women all the time, but somehow seeing Rose had set him back about a decade and a half. No, that wasn't true. When he was in high school, he hadn't had any trouble talking to girls. As the quarterback, he'd been one of the most popular guys around.

A lifetime ago.

He took the stairs down two at a time, made his way to apartment 114 and gave a loud knock. After a minute, he knocked even louder. This time, he heard movement and waited patiently for the door to open.

Mrs. Rubinski peered out at him through her thick glasses. She'd been his science teacher in seventh grade, and he'd thought she was ancient *then*. Her cat, Simone, wound herself through his legs, rubbing up against him as much as possible. He was convinced she did it so that when he had to go to Mr. Brown in 119, his dog Charlie would smell her scent all over him. Luckily, he had no intention of visiting Mr. Brown, or Charlie, today.

"You said your television wasn't working again, Mrs. Rubinski. I came to help."

Her green sweat suit was of the lime variety today. As long as he'd known her, Mrs. Rubinski and always worn green. All shades of green. Sometimes several different shades at the same time. Occasionally she would spice things up with a small bit of accent color. As in the orange turban she now wore. He tried not to stare.

She looked at her watch, but clearly didn't actually check the time. "It's about time, you said you'd be here ages ago."

He sighed. He'd told her an hour ago that he'd be there before six, to make sure she didn't miss the news. It had been four-thirty when he left his apartment to take Rose her plant, but he resisted the urge to look at his own watch or to correct her. It wouldn't make any difference.

She waved him towards the television set and he picked up the remote that was sitting on the side table. It only took three clicks to get the TV running the way she expected it to be, three clicks he'd shown her dozens of times, three clicks he could press in the dark, he'd done it so often.

"Thank you, dear. I'm going to talk to my son about helping me get a new television. It's a shame that this one breaks so often." She offered him a cookie from a plate sitting on her dining room table. He accepted gratefully. She made amazing cookies, always had.

"I think the television is fine, Mrs. Rubinski. I'm going to see if I can find you a different remote, one that will work better for you." One with a lot fewer options. "Thank you for the cookie, it's delicious, as always." He made his way to the door, but she followed him.

"I saw a moving truck. Who's our new neighbor?"

"Apartment 212," he told her. "Rose Chapman. You remember her, from my year?"

"Of course. Rose was always a sweet girl. We've hardly seen her back since she went away to college. Seems like she should have been visiting her parents more often than that."

He'd avoided Rose the first time she'd come back, and simply missed crossing her path the other times. He didn't offer any opinion on the matter and managed to extricate himself with only a few more swipes of cat hair to his pants and the thought, *when might he see Rose again?*

CHAPTER TWO

Rose and Naomi made good progress on the unpacking and didn't stop until the pizza they'd ordered arrived. She suspected that the young lady who delivered it was someone she'd babysat, as the girl looked familiar, but she couldn't quite place her and decided not to ask. She'd just feel old that she'd forgotten. They opened a bottle of wine and set up her tablet to video call Janelle, so they could see her and chat over dinner.

When they connected, Janelle got the salad she'd already prepared out of the fridge and sat down to eat with them.

"How was the drive? The car was okay?" Janelle asked.

"The car was perfect, thank you so much for doing the tune-up before I left. I'm going to miss you, of course, but I think my car is going to miss you even more. You babied it so well."

"Well, it was nice of you to let me practice on it when I was first learning the car stuff, so it was a win-win for both of us."

Rose laughed. "I'm pretty sure I got the best end of that deal, but you're welcome, too. Anyway, the drive was good. We saw some pretty landscapes."

"We are *so* up in the mountains," Naomi added. "I mean, I knew we would be, Colorado and all that, but these are for-real mountains."

Rose and Janelle laughed with her.

"Yeah, California's mountains are fun, but not quite the same," Rose agreed.

"Oh," Janelle said around a mouthful of food, waiving her fork around while she hastily chewed and swallowed. "Guess who called me at ten this morning to ask me why I hadn't booked him a reservation at the resort in Big Bear?"

"I'm going to guess Tony the Asshole," Naomi said before taking a bite of her pizza.

Tony was Janelle's boss, who she'd worked for since college.

"Yeah. So, I ask him, what are you talking about? And where are you, you have a meeting in twenty-five minutes. And he says he's in Big Bear, duh. He said he left me a voicemail yesterday to book him a suite at the resort, and he's pissed I didn't do so. I told him he hadn't, and that when I spoke to him yesterday afternoon and reminded him about his appointment this morning, he'd assured me he remembered."

Rose shook her head. It constantly amazed all of them that Tony the Asshole had managed to run a successful business, and make a lot of money doing it, for years before Janelle came along. "How long is he in Big Bear for?" she asked.

"A week. Said they'd gotten good snow and he wasn't going to miss the opportunity to ski."

"How nice for him. But at least it gives you a break from him."

Janelle nodded while she took a sip of her water. "Have you seen your parents yet?"

Rose shook her head. "No, I think we'll go to the hardware store in the morning, though. I need to get cleaning supplies, and I might as well do it there and get the family discount. And if I do that and see my dad, I'll have to go by Mom's house and see her, too, or she'll get pissy."

"And we can take like five minutes for her to show me around town, while we're out there," Naomi added. "That's all the time it'll take for her to show me everything."

Laughing, Rose agreed. "Yep, that's about right."

Naomi's phone beeped and she checked it, then rolled her eyes. "This clown is not getting the message."

"That guy you went on a date with last week?" Janelle asked.

"Yep. I'm about to block his number."

"How come you haven't yet?" Rose asked.

"I was giving him half a chance. If he handled the slow-down message well, I would have considered giving him a full second chance. But now he's just whining. Pathetic." She pushed the phone aside.

"What about you, Nell? Did you set a date with that internet guy yet?" Rose asked.

Janelle winced. "No. And I decided I'm not going to. I think he's homophobic. He's made a couple small remarks that rub me the wrong way."

"You're sure you're not seeing something that's not there, so you have an excuse to drop him?" Naomi asked, raising her eyebrows at the tablet.

"I'm sure."

"All right then."

"Are you going to look for more matches on the website?" Rose asked.

Janelle wrinkled her nose. "No, I don't think so. But my mom said she's setting me up with her chiropractor, so we'll see if he actually calls."

"Wait," Naomi said, putting down the slice of pizza she'd been about to bite into. "Has this guy seen your mother naked?"

Rose was taking a sip of her wine and choked at that. Naomi patted her back helpfully while Janelle laughed on the other end of the line.

"No, her chiropractor has not seen her naked," Janelle finally managed to answer.

"All right, fine, what do I know?" Naomi said and picked her slice back up.

IN THE MORNING, they had bagels and cream cheese from the supplies they'd packed in the car. Deciding it would be a good idea to hit the grocery store after the hardware store and visiting her mom, they headed out. It was snowing lightly, so they bundled up. Rose wondered how long it would take her to get used to this kind of weather again. She'd never become a sun bunny, even living in Los Angeles. She enjoyed going to the beach occasionally, but not often. The crowds, the sand, the threat of skin cancer, were all too much for her. But she wasn't a skier, either.

"Ooh, can we make snow angels?" Naomi asked.

Laughing, Rose grabbed her arm and dragged her through the parking lot. "We're going to need a bit more fresh snow for that, I'm afraid."

Naomi pretended to pout. "Fine. But at least I got to wear my cute hat."

She did look cute, in her green jeans, black down jacket and green beanie with a white pompom on top. Rose looked down at her considerably less stylish blue jeans, long-sleeved white t-shirt and gray down vest. And she wasn't wearing a hat at all, so her hair was just getting wet. She hurried them across the street to Hammerhead Hardware.

"Too bad it's not the Starbucks right across the street," Naomi said.

"That's just around the corner, we can stop there on our way to the grocery store."

The bell on the door chimed as they walked in, and she felt a surprising stab of nostalgia. She didn't see any customers, but she did see her mother.

"Mom, hey, what are you doing here?" She started around the counter to give her mother a hug.

"Really, Rose. I haven't seen you in a year, you don't bother to come see me when you get into town, and you walk into my own store and act surprised to see me." She gave an exaggerated sniff.

The last was said as they hugged. Rose refrained from mentioning that, as far as she knew, her mother hadn't worked in the store in over a decade.

"I'm sorry Mom, I'm a terrible daughter and you deserve so much better."

Her mother rolled her eyes and stepped back.

Naomi stepped forward and offered her own hug. "Hi, Francine. It's nice to see you again. This is your store?"

Her mom had come out to Los Angeles several times to visit, and had gotten to know Naomi and Janelle pretty well.

"Yes, mine and Rose's father's. We took it over from my father a few years before Rose was born."

"When did you start working here again?" Rose asked, still trying to wrap her brain around it.

"Last year. We split the week. I work Sunday, Monday, Tuesday and the mornings on Wednesday. He does Wednesday afternoon, Thursday, Friday and Saturday. That way we're both only working part-time."

Sounded smart to her, she was just shocked they'd come to an agreement. "That's great, Mom."

"Speaking of working, Alex, who works on weekends, is going on vacation this week. You can have those hours if you'd like."

"Um. Thanks, but I took this past week off for the move, so I'll be catching up this week, and probably need the weekend to finish settling in."

"Did you get another job? I know you said you have your web work to get you by, but you can't be lax in looking for a real job after being laid off. Employers like to see a consistent work history."

Rose forced in a deep breath. And then another. "Mom, I didn't get laid off. I quit, because my own business is doing well enough to support me on its own. It's computer based, but I make decent money. Thanks for thinking of me, though."

Her mom just shook her head, clearly not understanding a word Rose said. "I don't understand your generation. Computer jobs and internet stars and all that craziness. I offered Ethan Woodford the hours, and he turned me down as well."

Rose's sigh must have come out a little more sharply than she'd intended, because her mother glared at her. "Ethan is the manager at my apartment building. Maybe that's a full-time job. If he turned it down, it's probably because he doesn't need it."

"I know you liked him back in high school, Rose, but don't let his handsome face fool you. We hired him after you graduated, and I swear two weeks didn't go by before that boy was coming in late or calling out sick. He was a good worker when he was here, but we had to let him go after a few months. I thought I would be nice and give him a second chance." Her mom started sorting some screws she had in a bucket as she spoke.

"Wait. What? He didn't go to college in Denver? I thought he had a football scholarship."

"He didn't go. I think he's afraid of commitment. He's never had a long-term relationship. Heck, didn't he stand you up for prom?"

Somehow still embarrassed by that, Rose found herself shuffling her feet and forced herself to stop. "He didn't stand me up. He canceled. At the last minute."

"The same day. See what I'm telling you?"

"Okay, well, I need to get some cleaning stuff and get back to organizing the apartment. Do you want to come over for dinner next week, when I get everything settled?"

"Sure, honey, that would be lovely. Why don't you two come over tonight, so you don't have to cook after all your work?"

"Thanks, that sounds great. Just text me when you want us there."

She gathered the things she needed and brought them to the register. Her mom rang her up, applied the family discount, and accepted her credit card for payment, then sent them on their way.

The snow was falling more heavily when they left the store and she wondered if she should get winter tires. Winter was almost over and it seemed a terrible waste of money, especially when she could walk to most places in town, but an accident would be even worse. She'd ask her mom her opinion at dinner. Or Ethan, if she saw him first.

"I would have thought your mom would be super excited for you to be coming home," Naomi said as they headed to Starbucks.

"Yeah, she's been a little weird. I'm not sure what's going through her head. She's not an idiot, she understands the concept of being an entrepreneur, so I don't know why she refuses to understand I'm running a business, too."

"Maybe she's hoping you'll stay long-term, but afraid to say that since you got the short lease."

"Hm. Maybe." Her mom wasn't usually afraid to say what she was thinking, but she also wasn't one to push Rose too much. Her parents hadn't tried to discourage her when she'd told them she was determined to go to UCLA.

You could always ask her." Naomi reached past her to open the door and usher Rose inside.

"Yeah." Deciding to put those thoughts on the back burner for now, she texted her dad who said he was in the city picking up supplies and would catch her later in the day. They got their coffee and headed to the grocery store.

Rose was picking out lettuce when Naomi bumped her shoulder.

"I just spent three minutes getting a weather report from the dude by the garlic. I didn't ask about the weather. I didn't ask anything. I just smiled at him. That might have been my mistake."

Rose glanced over. "Mr. Anderson. He used to work at the pharmacy. We'd sit at the soda fountain counter and have flavored sodas in the summer. And ice cream."

"An actual soda fountain counter. Like in the paintings?"

"Yep, little stools that swiveled and everything. You could catch up on a lot of gossip there, with the kids at the counter and the adults hanging out. I think Mr. Anderson prided himself on never indulging in the gossip himself, so he maybe became expert about talking about the weather instead."

"Huh. Okay." Naomi moved off to look at the onion selection.

In the beans aisle, they ran into someone Rose recognized.

"Lucy, hey, how have you been?" she asked the younger woman as she reached for the pinto beans. Lucy had been three years behind her in school, so they hadn't been friends, but they'd lived only a couple of blocks away from each other so had often played together, with the other neighborhood kids.

"Rose, I heard you were coming back to town, how wonderful to see you!"

Lucy wrapped her arms around Rose, which gave Rose a chance to blink at Naomi in surprise. Apparently, Lucy had developed some sort of accent since they'd last spoken.

"Yeah, at least for a while. Or, heck, maybe permanently, I'm not sure yet."

"Well, welcome home. I'm working over at Quail's Nest restaurant now, so come in for a bite."

"I'll do that. How do you like it there?"

Lucy managed a Gallic shrug. "It's workable, for now, but I want to move over to Monarch. They opened a couple of years ago, upscale, excellent, much more what I'd like to be doing."

"Wow, that's great, at least there are several options in town, now."

"Yes, much better than when we were in school. But I'm surprised you'd come back. Was Los Angeles not working out for you?"

The weird accent was getting to Rose, and she wasn't sure she was projecting the condescending tone in the innocent words or not.

"Oh, it was great. I used it all up though, so it was time to move on," she said blithely.

She heard Naomi mostly suppress a snort.

"Anyway, I need to get back to unpacking, but I'll see you soon, I'm sure."

"It was nice to see you again, Rose."

As they walked away, Rose turned to Naomi. "Was I rude?"

"No."

"Was she rude?"

"A little bit. But more importantly, why does she sound like that?"

Rose giggled, glancing around to make sure they couldn't be overheard. "I haven't got a clue. She didn't use to."

They finally made it to the check-out counter, where they spent a couple more minutes chatting with the cashier, who had been a kindergarten teacher when Rose was a kid, though not hers.

When they got back to the apartment, they played music, worked hard and had the place pretty much fully together by the time her mom texted to say dinner would be ready in an hour.

"How about I call my dad and see if he's back and wants to meet up with us at the bar for a beer and a game of darts after dinner?" Rose asked. "You can experience the exciting nightlife before you head home tomorrow."

"Sounds like a plan. I need to see what options are out there before I decide if I should push you to make a move on the delicious Ethan Woodford."

Rose frowned. "I don't think so. Didn't you hear my mom?"

"Uh, yeah. Right after I heard her insult your successful business. So excuse me if I don't have a lot of confidence in her read on people. Didn't you say Ethan handled your lease arrangements just fine? And didn't he show up here with a plant for you, within two hours of your arrival?"

Laughing, Rose gave in. "Okay, you're right. I won't judge him based on anything Mom said."

"For now, going just by his appearance, I'd say he's a serious contender, but we'll check out the competition tonight."

"He did look pretty good, right? I mean, in high school he was fit, a total athlete. But as a grown man, *ooh baby*." And it was true. When she'd turned around and seen the adult version of Ethan Woodford, she'd wanted to lick her lips. He might not be an athlete anymore but she had no complaints about the way he filled out his shirt. The long sleeves had been pushed up and she'd wanted to grab on to his forearms.

"Uh, yeah, pretty good. And he definitely liked what he saw of grown up Rose."

"You think?"

Naomi just gave her a look. "Now, who gets the shower first?"

Rose looked out the window. "I think there's enough snow for angels. We should do that before showers."

"All right!"

They grabbed their phones and spent fifteen minutes playing in the snow and taking pictures before heading back into the building, laughing so hard they had to help each other up the steps.

When they were safely inside, Rose waved Naomi towards the shower. "You go ahead, and I'll call my dad."

She turned the music down and made the call.

"My girl! You're here! Are you getting settled in? Anything I can do to help?"

"We've pretty much got me all squared away, thanks. The movers you recommended were fantastic. We're going over to Mom's for dinner in a little while. Want to meet us at Wolfhound Tavern for a drink and a game of darts? Around eight?"

"That sounds like a perfect plan. I'll see you then. Have a nice dinner with Mom."

Naomi had gone through Rose's closet by the time Rose got out of the shower and picked out a couple of outfits.

"Holy crap, I am not wearing leather pants in Wildlife Ridge!"

"You look hot in these pants. Doesn't matter what city you're in."

"Okay, well, I am definitely not wearing them to dinner at my mother's house."

Naomi sighed and took the pants away, leaving Rose's tightest pair of jeans. She pursed her lips and considered. They really did make her ass look great. But, her dad was going to be there. Although she was pretty sure he wouldn't stay long. And the jeans did look fantastic with the top Naomi had picked out. It was a satiny purple wrap blouse, with long sleeves, so she shouldn't get too cold. It had been marked down twice, making it a great price.

They got dressed, Naomi looking super stylish in black jeans and a mustard sweater with a cowl neck and kickass gray boots. They pulled on their coats and headed out the door.

CHAPTER THREE

Ethan was chatting with his friend Ian Rabbit, who was playing bartender. Ian was manager at Wolfhound Tavern, which was owned by his uncle, but was filling in for one of his employees. Ian was telling him about a date he'd had in the city, in between serving drinks to the customers. It was a slow story-telling process, but not too bad as it was a Sunday night.

Ian headed back towards him after handing off the martini he'd been making, but his attention was on the door. Ethan looked over his shoulder and spotted Rose and her friend Naomi walking in. Rose was shrugging off her coat and hanging it on one of the hooks by the door, giving him a lovely view of her backside. He quickly turned around.

Ian had his head cocked in thought. "I know one of them, right?"

"Rose," Ethan told him. "From my year. Her friend Naomi is visiting to help her get moved in. She's at Salmon Springs."

"Wow, I'm surprised she's moving back, I think she's only visited two or three times since graduating."

"I let her have a six-month lease. She's not sure how long she's going to stay."

Ian got hailed to the other end of the bar, so Ethan walked over to the table Rose and Naomi had claimed.

"Ladies, can I buy you *welcome back* and *welcome to* drinks?"

Rose smiled and opened her mouth to reply but she wasn't as fast as Naomi, who hopped up. "That would be very nice, thank you. I'll come check out what's on tap. Rose, you want your usual?"

"Yes, please. And thank you, Ethan, that's sweet."

He followed behind Naomi, who leaned against the bar to read the taps. "What do you prefer?" he asked.

"I'm feeling like an IPA, I think."

"Then I suggest this one," he said, pointing to a recent addition to the bar that he favored.

"Sold." She transferred her attention to Ian as he walked over, giving him a stunning smile.

Ian seemed struck dumb, and Ethan nearly laughed out loud. "Ian, this is Naomi, visiting from California. Naomi, Ian runs the bar."

She held out a slim hand and Ian quickly wiped his on the towel hanging from his belt before taking her hand gently. "It's very nice to meet you, Naomi. What do you think of our little town?"

"Well, it's beautiful. I've never spent time in such a small town before. We haven't had a chance to do much besides get Rose moved in, so this is my first opportunity to really get out and see what it's like. This place is certainly nice. I like that the slight rustic mountain vibe is charming, but isn't taken too far."

Ethan glanced around the large space. The lights were low, but not too low, just as they should be for a neighborhood bar. The pool table and dartboard were on one side, near where Rose had gotten a small table. The opposite side held several larger tables, where people generally sat if they were going to order food. The bar was a long U-shape that held quite a few stools.

"Thanks," Ian said. "We updated a few years ago, removed all of the stuffed animal heads."

Ethan almost laughed as he could see Naomi trying to decide if she believed Ian or not. Ethan nodded and she shuddered.

"Good call. I approve."

He turned to Ian. "I told the ladies I'd get them drinks to celebrate the successful move."

"Rose will have a Long Island Iced Tea and Ethan's recommended this Pine Needle," Naomi told Ian.

"Good choice. Just give me a minute."

Naomi turned around to survey the bar, glancing over at him as she did so. "I'm impressed with how many people are here for a Sunday night."

"We're a foodie town, I think, and this place has some good bites. And winter's winding down so folks are feeling like getting out of the house. Bit of cabin fever, I guess. We get people who are vacationing in the cabins between here and the city, so they'll come in if they want signs of life. Same for the campers at the park."

She nodded, then glanced towards the door that had just opened again. "There's Rose's father. We're going to play darts."

"Nice. Did you go see the hardware store?"

"We did," she said as Ian returned with the drinks. "Francine was working, so we got to chat with her for a bit, and then we had dinner with her before coming over here."

"Do you know what George Chapman drinks?" Ethan asked Ian.

"Sure, he'd take a bottle of Bud."

"Grab me one of those, too, then. Thanks, Ian."

Drinks in hand, they made their way back to the table, which Ethan was alarmed to see Rose was banging her head on.

"Wow, we missed some fun, I guess," Naomi said.

Sitting up straight, Rose just shook her head.

"It's nice to see you, George," Naomi said as he stood to give her a hug.

"Naomi, it's been forever. I was sorry to miss you last time I was in Los Angeles."

Ethan handed over the drinks and Rose invited him to sit.

"Why were you banging your head, and not to the music?" Naomi asked.

"Dad wanted to let me know that Mom told him about me losing my job, and wanted to make sure I knew he was here for me if I needed any help."

"I thought I was being nice," George added, looking a bit peeved.

"It *was* nice, Dad. Thank you. But I didn't lose my job. I quit one job, because my business is doing so well I don't need it anymore. I would have thought Mom, being a small-business owner, would understand me being an entrepreneur."

"Ah. Well. You know your mother."

"Yes. She makes the most negative connotation possible of any conversation, and then refuses to believe that's not what you said."

"Well, I think she's more concerned about you coming back here, where it can be difficult to find a job." He held up a hand to stop her as she made to respond. "I know you have a job, and she knows you do, too, but the internet stuff is kind of ethereal to her and she's not convinced you can survive on it."

"Hm."

"But she's glad you're here," he assured her.

"You guys seem to have gotten a lot more friendly lately."

"Of course, why wouldn't we be?" He didn't wait for her to answer. "Anyway. I'm glad to hear your business is doing so well. I assume you've considered things like medical insurance, employment taxes and retirement accounts?"

"I have, yes. Have you?"

George laughed. "I'm sorry, honey, don't be insulted. You'd be shocked how many people try to run their own business and haven't considered those things. And I'll admit, your mother and I didn't for the first few years. It took us a while to figure things out properly. If we hadn't been running an already-established business, we probably wouldn't have lasted long." He took a drink of his beer and pointed at Ethan. "You remember, Ethan, that guy who tried to put a doggie daycare center in where the deli is now?"

Ethan smiled. "Yeah, word is he'd never heard of quarterly estimated taxes, and things didn't go well for him."

"So," Naomi said, raising her eyebrows at him. "Sounds like

George and Rose have their retirement plans in hand, how about you?"

"Naomi," Rose said with a groan. She shook her head at her friend and shot an apologetic look at Ethan.

"Oh, no," Naomi told Rose. "You know we don't play like that. Half the reason this country is such a mess as far as debt and savings is because people were taught not to talk to each other about money."

Rose sighed. "You're right." She looked at Ethan and shrugged. "She's right."

Ethan nodded. "I have it in hand as well. If you do, too, I'd say our table is definitely an anomaly."

Laughing, Naomi clinked her glass against Rose's. "He's not wrong. And this beer he suggested is excellent. You should keep him around, he's handy."

"Aw, shucks," he said, glad his blush wasn't visible.

Luckily, George, possibly taking pity on Ethan, jumped in.

"You said you girls got everything settled in the apartment? Need me to do anything?"

"I think I'm set, Dad, thanks. It's a nice space, Ethan. I'd never been in there before. It looks like it's been updated at some point?"

"Yes, we did a long, slow renovation so we didn't have to disturb most of the renters. Starting about six years ago, anytime someone moved out, I did a full rehab on their unit. Then I worked with a few of the old-timers. They would stay in one of the newly renovated units for a couple of weeks, at no charge, while I did theirs. It worked out well. A little grumbling now and then, but everyone was pretty happy with the results."

"Must have been pricey," George commented.

Ethan nodded. "Yes, but it had to be done to stay current. Before that, there hadn't been any real updates for about twenty years. I was able to raise the rents on new leases without affecting the old leases much. And the new renters didn't balk at the pricing, it's still competitive to what they're used to in the city or wherever they moved in from."

"Well, it turned out really well, I think," Rose said. "We were going to play darts, do you want to join us for a game?"

He checked his watch. It wasn't quite seven-thirty, he had a little bit of time. "I'd love to stay for a round."

They picked out their darts, George and Naomi fussing through the selection until they had three they liked. Rose and Ethan just grabbed the first three they could reach.

George wrote their names on the chalkboard, putting Naomi first in line, and gestured for her to go ahead.

She found the throw line with her right foot, moved back a hair, rolled her shoulders, wiggled herself into position, made a few practice motions, and threw—hitting just outside the bullseye and scoring twenty-five points. She did a little victory shimmy while Rose gave a cheer.

While Naomi made a couple more practice moves, Rose aimed an amused expression his way, and he grinned. She'd grown up so damn pretty. He remembered when he'd suddenly noticed her as a woman, their senior year in high school, rather than as the girl he'd known his whole life. He'd been walking down the hall and had heard her laughing. Glancing over, he'd caught sight of her, head thrown back, hand on her heart, face lit with joy over whatever her friend had said.

That's when he'd decided to ask her to prom. And he'd done just that. Only to disappoint her shortly after.

Reality had a way of biting him in the ass, and right now, it was reminding him that pretty women wanted more from a man than he could provide.

She gave him an odd look, so he supposed his own expression had changed. He shook his head to clear his thoughts and smiled, gesturing towards the board, as it was now her turn. Naomi had scored a double ten and a triple five.

"Can you beat her?" he asked.

"Not a single chance in hell," she answered, letting her grin come back out.

He watched as she quickly walked to the throw line and threw all three darts within seven seconds, taking about a millisecond to aim before each throw. She managed a five, a nineteen and a twelve, all clearly by accident.

His strategy was basically the same as hers, and he managed a triple four, a nine and an eleven.

George shook his head at the pathetic attempt. "Maybe you should go on that YouTube and see if you can find some tutorials on how to throw darts," he suggested, good naturedly.

"Dad!" Rose said with a laugh.

Ethan just smiled and shook his head.

George made his way to the line. He studied the board for a good fifteen seconds. Then he hefted one dart, fingered it, played with the…wings? Fins? Rudders? Whatever, George took a good few seconds to be sure it was how he wanted it, then returned to studying the board. Then, he moved, his arm coming up and the dart releasing in one fluid motion.

Bullseye.

The girls cheered and Ethan clapped. George gave a slight bow and repeated the process, this time hitting the twenty-five ring. His third shot only managed a six, though it landed just outside the center rings.

Naomi played another masterful round, and then Rose was up again. She was talking to her father, her face turned mostly towards him, when she took her first shot.

George groaned. "Honey, it would help quite a bit if you were actually looking at the target."

"Yeah, I'm not so sure about that," Rose teased. She threw again and, though she was looking at the board, managed to hit the wall an inch to its side.

"You did that on purpose," George accused.

"I did not!"

She was laughing, but Ethan still thought she was telling the truth.

Her last dart bounced off the metal divider between two of the numbers and they all pretended not to notice as she picked it up and threw again.

The game moved quickly, and Ethan enjoyed himself. He also managed to not check his watch too often, but as soon as George hit the game-winning score, he turned to Rose.

"I need to head out. Thank you for including me, that was fun."

"Thanks for the drink. And the welcome home." She gave him a hug, and Naomi did as well.

"I hope you come back to visit again, and stay longer next time," he told her.

"I'm sure I'll be back. It was nice to meet you, Ethan."

"I'll walk out with you," George said. "Let the girls have some fun without the old man hanging around."

Ethan went back to the bar to grab his coat and settle up with Ian, then met George as he was finishing saying goodbye.

The snow had stopped by the time they got outside. Winter was on its way out, though it liked to take its time in this part of Colorado.

He nodded at George and headed towards his truck, waiting until he was inside and the engine was going to check his phone. He had a text from his brother-in-law, making sure he'd be heading over to see his sister. As if he'd forget. He sighed and sent a quick response that he was on his way.

Jackson was working the late shift and didn't leave for the city until after an early dinner. Alyssa liked for Ethan to come over on the nights Jackson was working, but felt like she was imposing if he spent *too* much time there. He checked his watch. If he left now, he'd hit the sweet spot of neither too early, or too late.

He sent a text to Alyssa, letting her know he was about to leave and checking to see if she needed anything. Her reply that she only needed him made him smile.

Everyone always seemed to expect him to fail them, and yet wanted his help. But Alyssa, she just wanted to see him. And she never made him feel unappreciated when he gave her his time, and was careful not to ask too much of him. As if she, of all people, could.

Shaking off his irritation, he put the truck in gear. He had approximately six minutes to decide if he was going to tell Alyssa about seeing Rose at the bar. By now, she'd likely have already heard Rose was back and living in his building. If he didn't mention playing darts with her at the bar, she'd hear about it later and wonder why he was keeping it to himself. If he did, she might bring up senior prom, and that wasn't something he wanted to deal with.

He still hadn't decided by the time he pulled up to her driveway, so he was going to have to wing it. Walking into the warm house that was so very Alyssa, he smiled. It smelled delicious, which was an excellent sign that she'd had a good day, but also meant he had to make sure she hadn't overdone it and tired herself out too much.

He hung his coat on the coat rack that looked like a piece of modern art, then headed down the teal hallway with bright paintings on the walls. He found Alyssa settled in on the couch, a Hallmark Christmas movie playing on the television, which was good. If she'd been knitting, he would have had to chastise her for overdoing it after cooking. There was no question that Jackson might have done the cooking. He was useless in the kitchen.

Alyssa paused the movie when he walked in, smiling at him over her shoulder.

"My favorite girl," he said, coming around the couch to kiss her cheek.

"Proof you need to get out more."

"Hey, I was just at the Wolfhound. Played darts with George and Rose Chapman, and her friend. You heard she's moving back to town for a while?"

"Yes. What I don't know is why I didn't hear that from *you*, since you must have talked to her about the apartment before she showed up."

"Landlord-tenant confidentiality?" he asked, taking a seat and stealing some of her afghan.

"Mm-hm. If you say so." She eyed him closely, but apparently decided not to pursue the topic further. "Don't get too comfortable, you should have stopped in the kitchen on your way to the living room."

"It does smell good. What did you make?"

"Grandma Patrice's gumbo."

He stood up immediately, throwing the blanket back and heading to the kitchen with the sweet sound of her laughter trailing him.

The pot was on the stove, waiting for him, with the container it was to be stored in sitting on the counter. He dished up a bowl and found it warm enough that he didn't need to reheat it. A large slice of bread from the bakery at Jackson's grocery store was also waiting for him. He put butter on it, stuck it in his mouth, grabbed a napkin from the counter, a bottle of beer from the fridge and a spoon from the drawer, then headed back to the living room.

Alyssa laughed again at the sight of him and pushed a couple of books out of his way on the coffee table. He put the bread on the napkin and went in for a taste of the gumbo. Flavor exploded over his tongue and he moaned out loud.

"You done good," he said after swallowing. "Grandma would be proud."

"Thanks, bro. I had a good day."

"I can tell." And he could. She had color in her cheeks and her eyes didn't look too sunken. It was days like this one that made him think she would beat the cancer. But these days were coming less and less often. And he refused to think about that.

"What's this movie you're watching?"

She described the sweet romance to him while he ate, catching him up to speed before turning it back on. When he put his empty bowl down, she snuggled into him, falling asleep not long afterward.

He didn't move, not for a long while, even after the movie finished, enjoying the sound of her even, unlabored breathing. Finally, he nudged her awake before lifting her in his arms and carrying her to the bathroom. He held still until she was steady on her feet, then waited for her to do her thing and shuffle to her bed. He had the covers down and ready and checked to see that the glass of water on the bedside table was full.

She slipped into bed and rolled to her side, hand under her cheek, blinking at him sleepily. "You didn't need to stay so late."

"I had to see how the movie ended."

She rolled her eyes, which looked funny sideways.

"Go home. You need rest, too."

"Yes ma'am."

"Love you, bro."

"Love you, Lyssie."

CHAPTER FOUR

The drive to take Naomi to the airport was just over two hours. They called Janelle on her lunch break and chattered away until the other woman had to get back to work. They listened to music and got a little weepy as they discussed plans for Naomi and Janelle to come visit in a few months.

She did some shopping before leaving the city and realized it was just about dinnertime as she wound her way back into Wildlife Ridge. She was considering stopping at Wolfhound Tavern since she hadn't been hungry enough to try the food the previous night, and it had looked good, but the phone rang. Seeing that it was her mom, she answered.

"Hey Mom. I'm just driving back into town."

"Oh, good, I knew you were taking Naomi to the airport but wanted to make sure you were home safe before it got too late. There's supposed to be some sleet tonight."

Okay, so it was a little weird to get this kind of mothering after having distance from it for sixteen years, but she could handle it.

"Yep, all safe and just considering what I want to do for dinner. Have you eaten?"

"No, but I have some nice chicken ready to fry up. You want to come by here and help me with that?"

That actually sounded pretty nice. "Sure, that would be great. I'll be there in a few minutes."

She hadn't spent much time in the house since she'd left for college. A few short visits was all she'd managed between being busy with college, starting a new job, and then launching her own side business.

Passing the street her apartment building was on, she continued to Beaver's Dam road. On the right was Lady Bug Park, the far end of which had a small lake that was great for fishing in the summer and ice skating in the winter. On the left were a couple of housing tracks. She turned down June Bug lane and pulled up to the house she'd spent her whole childhood in. Her parents had bought it the week they'd gotten married, with a little help from their own parents.

The house remained largely unchanged from when she'd moved out. Her father's favorite reading chair and lamp were gone, his fishing-themed artwork that had been in the den, and the copper pots and pans he'd loved to cook with were all gone, but she wondered why her mother hadn't redecorated. Was it finances? That had to be a big part of why her mom had gone back to work, but she wasn't sure if it was something she could bring up.

When she'd left for college, her mom had called her only a few weeks later, crying, about the divorce. Rose had been shocked. They'd never seemed the most romantic couple, but neither had they seemed unhappy. They hadn't fought much, not like some of her friends' parents did.

At first she'd been supportive of her mom—her dad pretty much refused to discuss it with her, simply saying that it was between him and her mother—but after a while it had gotten exhausting listening to the same sad complaints, call after call. And when her mom stopped mentioning him, she let it go and never brought him, or the hardware store, up again.

As she peeled the potatoes, she figured she'd start with the work end of things and see where that got her.

"I'm glad you and Dad have worked out the store situation. You hadn't mentioned that when we talked."

"I thought I had. It wasn't a big deal, I was bored and needed to be doing something. I'm too young to be retired. Speaking of young, I was thinking you should meet Mrs. McGee's son, Jeremy. You know her, right? The high school vice principal?"

"You told me in high school if you caught me talking to Jeremy, I'd be grounded for a month." Rose started cutting up the peeled potatoes while her mother heated the oil in the frying pan.

"That was different. He was four years older than you and already sleeping around."

"And not the least bit interested in me," Rose pointed out. "What's he up to these days?"

"Living in Colorado Springs, working at a micro-brewery. Manager, I think."

"Good for him." She put the potatoes into the water.

"So you don't want to go on a date with him?"

"I don't even know if I'm staying here long term, Mom. I just want to get my feet under me with doing my business full time, and I needed to get out of Los Angeles to make that work. I want to focus on that right now, and I don't think Jeremy's the type to play second fiddle to a woman's career goals."

Her mom frowned as she moved one piece of chicken through the breading process. "I suppose not, but you can't just put your romantic life on hold indefinitely. That's no way to get me grandbabies."

Rose laughed and kissed her mom's cheek. "I'll get around to that eventually. Probably. But this is a critical time for me."

"I'd believe that more if you had been dating up until now, but it seems to me it's been a while."

"Yeah. Well. You're not wrong. I just...guys are so annoying, really. You meet them and they seem pretty cool, and then two or three dates later you can barely recognize them from the first date."

"You haven't been serious with anyone since Dan, right?"

"Dan. Ugh. I guess that's about right. I mean, I've had, you know…" She glanced at her mother who kept her attention on the chicken. "Friends. But nothing serious since him. What a loser. I invite him to move in and suddenly he thinks I'm going to cook dinner all the time and do his freaking laundry? What's up with that? And it's not like we moved fast. We dated for nine months before I asked if he wanted to move in. Then, wham! Did a total one-eighty. My head spun."

"Some guys are like that, I guess, but—"

Now that she was on a roll, Rose couldn't stop. "I mean, seriously. Why do they do that? It's like with Dad. He was this perfectly normal husband all those years, and then he leaves you, no warning, no discussion. How is that okay?"

"Well, that's not—"

"I try not to think about it when I'm with him, 'cause he's my dad, but it seriously sucks that he would treat you like that after twenty years. How are we supposed to be with someone if we never know when they'll just completely change like that?"

Her mom frowned and washed her hands before turning to face Rose. "Is that what you think?"

"What do you mean?"

"That everything was fine one day and he just left the next?"

"Well, yeah. That's what you told me. When you were crying your heart out, totally shocked and betrayed that he would do that."

The stricken look on her mom's face had Rose taking a step forward. "Hey, what's wrong?"

"I don't remember doing that. I was upset, but I shouldn't have said that. I shouldn't have let you believe your father would do that."

"I—I don't get it. What happened, if not that?"

"Oh, honey. Normal life happened. We both grew in different ways. He wanted to expand the business, but I didn't think that was a good idea. He talked about opening another location, but I didn't want to risk what we had, risk my father's legacy. We argued, but we were careful not to do it in front of you. That's not why we split, it's just that we started to want different things and we were seeing the world in different ways. We drifted apart, and once you left, it just sort of…became not worth sticking it out anymore."

"But, you were so upset. You said you couldn't believe he'd do that to you, after all your years together. You said it was out of the blue." Rose just shook her head, trying to wrap her mind around what she was hearing. Her mom looked distressed, so she was trying to rein it in, but *damn.*

"I was upset. I probably did say those things. And I'm sure I meant them at the time, but I was being unfair to your father. I was scared of not being a team after twenty years, scared of being alone. I'm so sorry, I shouldn't have laid that stuff on you."

"Wow. I just…wow." Rose gestured to the oil. "Go ahead. I'll get the paper towels."

She lined a plate with towels while her mom started putting chicken pieces into the hot oil.

"Do you date?" she asked, shocked to realize she'd never considered the possibility.

Her mom gave her a side-eyed look, as if considering her response.

"It's okay. I'm good either way."

"I was seeing a cook from the Sit A Spell diner for a couple of years."

"Wow."

"He's divorced too, grown children too, and we enjoyed spending time together, but neither of us was interested in taking it past that. Then he met a woman from Denver and they fell in love. I was happy for him. I miss being with someone, but not him specifically."

She chewed on her lip while she turned the chicken, and Rose got the impression there was more.

"Mom…" She dragged the word out.

"I was thinking of asking your father if he wanted to go see *Wicked* when it comes to the city. You know he loves musicals, but I can't imagine he'd go see one on his own. And I don't think he's seeing anyone."

Rose just stared. And blinked. And stared some more. Talk about her world doing a one-eighty.

"But we have a good thing going, with being friendly towards each other and working the hardware store together. I don't know if I want to risk that."

"What does Belinda say?" Rose asked. The head librarian at Wildlife Ridge Library had been her mom's best friend since elementary school.

"She says sometimes people grow apart, but it's just as easy to grow back together."

"Hmm. She probably has a pretty good sense for it. She pays attention to things and is good at seeing the whole picture." Rose held the plate out for her mother to put the chicken on, then patted it with more paper towels.

"True. I'm sorry about the phone calls when we were getting divorced. I shouldn't have done that. I think it was easy to play the victim over the phone, and wallow in the worst aspects of it, but it was wrong. I didn't mean to make your dad out to be the villain."

"I know. I understand." She kissed her mom's cheek and took the pot to the sink to dump the potatoes into the colander.

"Do you think that's why you haven't had any longer-term relationships?" her mom asked, sounding hesitant.

"No, I think it's more about losers like Dan. Or, you remember my friend Jennifer? Her husband, Matt, lost his job like two months after their wedding, and just became a total freeloader. None of us could believe it, to be honest. Spent all day smoking pot and playing video games, barely even pretending to look for a new job." She paused while using the mixer to mash the potatoes. When she'd switched it off, she continued. "Or, you know, maybe I just haven't met the right guy."

Her mom added butter and milk, and Rose turned the mixer back on. When the potatoes were smooth and creamy, they made up their plates, adding salad that her mom had already mixed together, and sat at the table.

After they'd eaten a few bites, her mom looked at her seriously. "Don't let a few bad examples sour you on relationships. Being in a happy, healthy partnership is one of the best things in life. I want that for you. And kids. Nothing I've done in my life has meant more to me than helping create a wonderful human being like you."

Her throat closed up and she had a hard time swallowing her piece of chicken. "Mom."

"I'm just saying."

"I love you."

"I love you, too. Now eat before it gets cold."

CHAPTER FIVE

As she went through her nighttime routine, Rose debated how she wanted to start the next morning, her first official workday as a woman working solely for herself. She could either embrace the freedom and not set an alarm clock, or she could set the alarm for a "normal" workday and keep to a routine.

She decided to try the freedom route, figuring she wasn't going to sleep in very late, even without the alarm, so it didn't really matter. Getting a glass of water from the kitchen, she took her vitamins while thinking about the fact that she'd met her big life goal. At some point in the near future, she was going to need to sit down and write her next big goals. She had some ideas, but she'd found that actually writing them down made all the difference, even if the goals ended up changing later.

Setting her glass in the dishwasher, she turned to the desk she'd set up in the corner of her living room. She'd given herself the view of the mountains and wondered if that had been a mistake. Would she just stare out the window when she was trying to work? She was used to either working in an office surrounded by other people chatting or clicking away, or working at home at night. Well, the weekends, also, but her apartment in Los Angeles didn't have room for a desk and a dining table, so she'd switched to the desk once she'd decided to make a full press on her business. And the view had been of the front door of another apartment.

She sat at her desk. Maybe it was time for a new chair? She'd be spending a lot of time in this chair, now. She'd gotten it second hand years ago and it had served her well. But now wasn't the time to go on a spending spree. Well, never was the time to go on a spending spree, really, but she would add a line item to her budget for a new office chair, set it up so that she could get a good quality one in a year or two, if she was ready by then.

Deciding to go ahead and do that now, since she wasn't feeling particularly sleepy, she pulled up her financial software. Then she decided she'd better research chairs a bit, so she'd know what amount she wanted to shoot for. After half an hour, her head was spinning and she decided to just overestimate and worry about the details later. And since her chair really was fine, she decided later meant two years, not one, so she divided her total by twenty-four months and plugged it in. Playing with the numbers absorbed her for a while, as it tended to do, and she realized it was midnight when she pushed back from the computer. And that she'd just spent a significant amount of time obsessing about something totally unimportant, rather than freaking out about the fact that for the first time in her adult life, she would not be getting a paycheck at the end of two weeks of work.

Damn it, she had this. She'd worked hard, and *knew* she was going to succeed. Tomorrow she would start proving it.

She sent a quick group text to Naomi and Janelle, then slid into bed. Once again, she debated on the alarm clock issue. She needed to find the right balance between not being stuck in a nine-to-five grind, but taking her own business seriously. Not that anyone could accuse her of not taking it seriously. She'd been working nearly full-time hours on her so-called side gig, in addition to her full-time job. She'd needed to do it, to build her contacts, reputation and portfolio, in addition to her savings fund. She'd set a goal of what it would take to quit the day job and now she was here.

She grinned into the dark. The girls had treated her to a champagne dinner at Janelle's to celebrate, even though it had meant she'd be moving after giving her notice at work. They'd made different goals than her, and were so close, as well. She couldn't wait to celebrate their milestones with them.

WHEN SHE BLINKED her eyes open, Rose saw that it was only ten minutes past the time her alarm would normally be set to go off. Not bad. She was actually ahead of the game, since she didn't need to factor in commute time. She debated between showering and dressing right away, or going the yoga pants route. It was sort of a silly debate, it wasn't like she hadn't spent many, many weekends working in her yoga pants, but today was a Monday so she decided to stick with tradition and get properly dressed.

Feeling all kinds of adultish, she even swiped on a bit of lip gloss and mascara before sitting at her computer and pulling up her emails. She'd just started her first response when her phone rang. It was her mom, asking if she wanted to drive with her to Costco after work. Although annoyed at the interruption, Rose had to admit it was a good idea, and it would be more fun to make the hour-and-a-half-long trip to Denver with company, so they made the plan.

Rolling her shoulders, Rose went back to work. Except, she got distracted by Twitter.

Which somehow led her to Facebook.

She frowned at her computer. She never had those programs open at work, though unless she was on a tight deadline, she did have them open at home. But that was then, and this was now, and now *this* was the real work, so she should turn those programs off and leave them for actual leisure time. Which she would have, now that she wasn't working two jobs.

Right. Close, close, and back to work. She decided emails could wait until later, and lost herself in the coding. This is what she loved to do.

When she looked up and realized it was three and she'd barely moved from her chair once, she pushed her keyboard in and stood. Her body was sore and achy, which was ridiculous, she hadn't spent nearly as much time in front of the computer as she'd done when she was working a forty hour week for an employer, and then nearly that many again for her own business, but she was usually better at moving around a bit.

She stood at the sink, staring out her window as she ate a microwave burrito. A man walked his dog down the sidewalk, and she wondered if she should get a dog. Except, that would not work with her plans to be able to get up and move whenever and wherever she wanted. At least, she thought most countries had quarantine rules. Maybe she should research that. At any rate, she didn't actually need a dog to take a walk. Standing at a sink to eat a burrito was not a proper lunch break. Taking a long walk would be, though, even if it was late in the afternoon. She put her plate in the sink, grabbed her jacket, and headed out.

It was a beautiful day, warmer than it had been, and most of the snow was melted away. The sky was a clear blue with sporadic white clouds to keep things interesting. Winter was almost done and she was ready for the beauty of a mountain spring.

So far, she'd only driven through town and run specific errands, she hadn't yet taken the time to walk around and explore the changes. It was such a charming little town, which, of course, she hadn't realized growing up. Only now, after having lived in Los Angeles for over a decade, did she appreciate the picturesque beauty. She went down the steps of the building, which put her on Dragonfly Road. She glanced across the street at the hardware store. It, like the realtor's office and the sporting goods store it was between, had started life as a house. One was slate blue, one sage green and the other a not-too-bright yellow. Her dad had mentioned that the three businesses had gotten together a few years ago to coordinate a new paint job. She couldn't see her dad unless she walked the wrong way, so she kept on. She stopped at the corner of Main Street to pet a collie who was coming out of the vet's office, chatting with the little girl on the other end of his leash and her dad. A trio of bicyclists zoomed by.

A lot of the buildings on Main Street were brick, some with colorful awnings. In the spring, she knew, there would be fresh flowers everywhere, in window boxes and planters pulled out of storage.

She poked her head into the library, but Belinda, her mom's best friend for as long as Rose could remember, was busy, so she only waved, figuring she'd come back and explore another time. If they had decent Wi-Fi and comfortable chairs, it might be nice to have a change of scenery sometimes when she was working.

She walked past the post office and the Starbucks, another possible work location to consider, and paused at the Quail's Nest Restaurant to look at the menu. It looked good for a decent, casual meal.

"There's our Rose, come back to us," she heard.

She turned and saw Walter Anderson exiting the restaurant. He hadn't seen her at the grocery store the day he'd spoken to Naomi.

"Mr. Anderson, it's so nice to see you."

"Now, I told you last time you were in town, you call me Walter."

"Okay, Walter. Thank you." She gestured to the street. "I haven't had a chance to walk around until now. A lot is the same, but some new stuff, too. I think this restaurant was a clothing store."

"It was, for a lot of years. Change is good, helps keep the town alive. And the food here's pretty good, too."

"I'll definitely give it a try. I was talking to Lucy the other day, she said she works here."

He reached up to take his Broncos ball cap off, run his hand over his nearly bald head, and replace the cap. She had to work hard not to smile.

"Lucy's a good girl, and works hard at the restaurant. Now, you don't stay out too long, the temperature's going to be dropping in a couple of hours. We'll have a bit of snow tonight."

"No, sir, I'm on my lunch break, I'll be heading back to work soon."

He tipped his hat to her and walked back the way she'd come.

She turned onto Elk Street, imagining how the park would look in the spring and summer. It started out narrow at Main Street, but then ballooned into a large park, with only the town hall at the end of it and several benches for people to sit and enjoy. Her first "date" had been on the wide lawn in front of the old colonial-style government building. It had been seventh grade and Harry Khalid had asked her out on a picnic. His mom and younger sister had sat on a blanket several yards away, while she and Harry had enjoyed the sandwiches he'd made and the lemonade she'd contributed.

Smiling at the memory, she walked the full circle back to Main Street, passing the junior and senior high school. The bell rang and suddenly kids were streaming outside, their excited freedom contagious.

Nodding at one of her neighbors who was coming out of the Sit A Spell diner, she reached the new antique store. Well, she wasn't sure how new it was, but she'd never been inside. A little bell tinkled as she went through the door. It was strange, going into shops like this on a weekday. There was no one else inside now, but when she'd passed by with Naomi during the weekend, it had been busy. One of the benefits of her freedom was that she should be able to hit the stores during the week, when they were less crowded, right?

So why did she feel guilty that she wasn't sitting at her desk right now?

She checked her watch. Still within the lunch hour. And besides, if she wanted a long lunch, that was totally allowable.

The problem was that she'd spent years running her business as a side job, around normal working hours, fitting in what time she could here and there, sacrificing sleep and free time. Now she didn't need to do that. She'd calculated things to be sure that she could support herself with a forty-ish hour workweek.

Shaking off her self-doubt, she focused on the store. A jean-clad butt backed its way in through a door on the far side of the store. After a couple of steps, she saw that the man was carrying one end of a console and was soon followed by another man, who caught sight of her and smiled.

"Sorry, have you been here long? We were just getting this beauty unloaded from the truck." His straight black hair hung in his eyes and he jerked his head a bit to clear them.

"No, I've only been in a minute, don't worry about me. I'm just looking around to be nosy, not actually shopping."

He set down his end of the console, and his companion did as well, then turned to greet her. Without doing anything overt, they fairly screamed "committed couple" to her. She had to admire the level of partnership that resulted in such obvious togetherness.

"I'm Cal and this is Jin. And we've been in Wildlife Ridge long enough to know that you're the Chapman girl, who left right out of high school and has been living in California." He said it with such an engaging grin that she couldn't help but laugh.

"Let me guess, you guys aren't from a small town."

Jin pouted, but his eyes were twinkling. "You can already tell? We've been here two years now, I thought we were getting the hang of it."

"It was the glee in Cal's voice when he knew who I was. Next time go for nonchalance," she suggested.

They nodded solemnly, then Cal winked at her.

"Well, how can we satisfy your curiosity today? Surely, as you've just moved in, you need something for your apartment."

She moved closer, studying the elegant wood console they'd carried in.

"Where do you find the pieces for the store?"

Cal took a cloth from his back pocket and polished where he'd been gripping the walnut. "Estate sales, mostly. People bring items, too, or call us to come out and take a look at what they have."

"Well, I'm afraid I'm in a minimalist phase right now, so it's lost on me, but you've got a lovely place."

An elderly man and woman walked in and Jin moved to greet them. Rose checked her watch. "I need to head back, I was just taking a break to wander the town a bit. I'm sure I'll see you guys around, and quiz you on how you've taken to small-town life."

Cal grinned. "We'll buy you a welcome-back cocktail or coffee and hold you to it."

She'd mostly reached the end of Main Street, with just a Burger King left, so she crossed the street and headed back. She passed the church and the strip mall that she noted still held the pizza parlor, the yoga studio. She and Naomi had shared an elevator ride with one of her neighbors who'd mentioned working at the yoga studio. She should check into taking a class. She made a mental note to look into that as she picked up her pace. She needed to get back to answer a few emails before it was time to pick up her mom for their Costco run.

ROSE'S DAYS began to pick up a rhythm she was happy with, although she had to continually remind herself that she could adapt and change as needed. Her new Wednesday routine was to take a long lunch break that included a trip to the grocery store, when it wasn't crowded.

She had three bags hanging from her hands as she made her way up the walk to the apartment building. Cocking her head, she studied the man sitting on the front steps. Ethan was wearing jeans and a flannel shirt open over a t-shirt that fit him like a second skin, in a way she very much appreciated. He was sitting on the top step, chin in his hand, gaze on hers.

"Did you need a break from your work, too?" she asked.

He gestured to a small area off to the side that she hadn't seen as she walked up. A small dog was playing with what looked like a stuffed animal. Worrying it and jerking it about.

"That's Ellie. Mr. Houston in 203 broke his leg a couple of weeks ago and Ellie hasn't had a chance to get out much, so I said I'd sit with her for a while.

Hearing her name, Ellie decided it was time to come greet the newcomer. She trotted up, stuffed animal held tightly in her mouth. She dropped the toy at Ethan's feet, then put her front paws on Rose's legs. She was tiny, couldn't be more than eight pounds. Rose's heart melted as the dog pawed at her until she set one bag down, bent and rubbed her tiny head.

The little sweetheart closed her eyes and wiggled gently under Rose's hand.

"Oh my, she's adorable." Scooping the dog up, she joined Ethan on the step and sat, the dog curling up in her lap and licking her hand until Rose resumed stroking her head.

"Mr. Houston. I think he used to live on our block."

"Yes. He retired from the sawmill a few years back and moved here. Said he wanted to cut expenses and not ever have to mow a lawn or shovel snow again."

She nodded and looked down at the dog. "Is this okay? Should I be letting her run around and getting her exercise?"

"She's fine. She'll get up in a minute and convince you to throw her snake."

Rose glanced over at the stuffed animal that had been abandoned on the ground. She supposed the bedraggled purple and teal thing could be a snake.

"So, you've been in town, what? Two weeks now?" Ethan leaned back on his hands. "Does it feel like you never left?"

She snickered. "Almost two weeks. And yes and no. On the one hand, yeah, Wildlife Ridge hasn't changed much. Except for the better food."

"But on the other hand, you've changed."

"Exactly. I mean, high school kid. I sure hope I've changed a lot."

Ellie started dancing around in Rose's lap, so she lifted the dog up to her face, gave her a kiss on her tiny nose, and set her on the ground. She immediately raced to the toy and picked it up, though it was nearly as big as she was. Prancing back to them, she offered the snake to Rose.

Rose tried to take it, but Ellie hung on, so they played tug of war.

"Did you like living in Los Angeles?" Ethan asked.

"Sure. It was a good place to go to college. There's always something happening. And I met some wonderful people. The diversity, the culture, the ability to go see *Rocky Horror Picture Show* one night and *Les Misérables* the next. I definitely enjoyed my time there, and wasn't sure how I'd take to coming back to small town life. In LA, you can have tons of friends and yet still be essentially anonymous."

"It's definitely hard to imagine that. Everybody is all up in everyone else's business."

"Yeah, but it can be a nice thing, too. I didn't even know most of my neighbors' names. Here, if you don't see your neighbor getting their mail at four-fifteen like they do every day, you knock on their door to make sure they're okay."

Ellie finally gave up on winning the game and released the toy. Sitting down, she watched Rose expectantly. Rose flung the snake ten feet, and the tiny dog raced after it with a couple of yaps.

"True. But don't tell me no one has tried to get up in your business." He narrowed his eyes at her while she fought off a blush. "Let's see...I'd bet at least two people have said something to you about me being single since you got back. Probably in the form of a warning to keep yourself clear."

She had to bite her lip to keep from laughing, but then gave in. "You do know your town. Three, actually. Lindsay Ringman saw me watching your butt when you left the deli the other day and told me not to get my hopes up, because you don't date."

"You were watching my butt?" He put his hand to his heart and looked shocked.

"Of course I was. It's even better than it was in high school, and I was pretty fond of it back then."

He laughed. "Um, thanks? And Lindsay's one to talk, she's been leading Carl Weiss on for months but won't commit. At least I'm honest about not being interested in a relationship."

"And why is that?" she asked as Ellie ran back up with the snake, ready for another round of tug. This time Rose pulled for a few seconds, then let go. Ellie raced away in triumph. "Nobody in Wildlife Ridge that interests you?"

He was quiet for long enough that she turned to scan his face. The serious expression gave her pause. She'd meant the question to be teasing. She almost retracted it, but he finally spoke.

"I should have apologized to you. I mean, I know I did back then, but it wasn't enough. It wasn't right, canceling on you for prom at the last minute. I hated it…and I didn't want to ever be in that position again."

Stunned, she just stared at him for several seconds until Ellie yapped at her. She looked down at the little pup and took the proffered toy, giving a gentle tug.

"Are you saying you haven't dated since high school?"

"A bit. After my mom died, I did. But I realized I'm not in a place where I can make a relationship my number one priority, and most women want to be that. Hell, they *deserve* to be someone's highest priority. So until I'm ready to give that, I don't want to be in a position of disappointing people like I did that day."

"Okay. I can see that. And I'm sure you've found women who agree, and are happy to…um…"

"Friends with benefits?" he suggested.

"Exactly."

"I've had enough friends, yes. It's not like I don't enjoy women, and being with them." He grinned. "And I do mean out of bed, as well as in."

She nodded. "That's where I've been the last several years, so I totally get it."

"Yeah?"

"Yeah, I was just telling Mom that's why she can't set me up on a date with Jeremy McGee. I didn't think he'd take to not being someone's first priority."

He snorted. "Agreed."

Ellie came back and he scooped her up. "I need to take her back. Keep me company back to Mr. Houston's, and I can offer you a cupcake from Trisha. I helped her out yesterday and she brought me half a dozen. They're freaking delicious, but I need help. Please. And I want to hear more."

She sighed. "What I do for my friends." She stood and brushed off her rear before opening the door of the building for him. The twinkle in his eye as he passed let her know he'd been watching her butt. She grinned as she followed him inside.

WHEN THEY'D RETURNED Ellie to her thankful owner, Ethan led Rose to his unit, trying to visualize what state it was in. He was pretty sure he hadn't left anything embarrassing out. He was a fairly tidy person, in general, but he hadn't expected company.

He opened the door and let her in, glancing around quickly to see that everything was pretty much in place. He dropped his keys on the table by the front door and headed straight for the kitchen, gesturing for her to take a seat at the little table. He put her grocery bags in the fridge.

"So," he said as he pulled down two small plates. "No dating for the last few years?"

"No dating with intent. Like you said, I go out with people, but we're clear that a commitment isn't the goal."

He opened the bakery box and added cupcakes to the plates, grabbed napkins and brought them to the table. "Did you have a bad breakup?"

She narrowed her eyes at him. "How come there has to have been a bad breakup? Would you ask a guy that question?"

"Are you saying the answer is no?" He cocked an eyebrow at her, holding back a smile as she wrinkled her nose. "Just as I thought."

He watched as she took her first bite of the lemon cupcake. She stuck her tongue out and delicately swiped a bit of the icing first, then moaned. He felt the sound deep in his gut.

She opened her mouth and took a full bite, eyes closing as she savored it. He watched her lips, then forced his gaze down to his own cupcake before his body started to react to the ideas that his imagination was sparking.

"Yes, I did have a bad breakup. But I also started my own business, while working full time. So I needed to make that my number one priority. Like you said, if you're in a relationship, the other person has a right to expect more from you. And I wasn't ready to give it."

"And now?"

"Now, even more so. I've just gone full time with my own business, and I need to focus on that to make sure it's a success."

"That makes sense." He ate the last bite of cupcake. "Do you want another one?"

"No, thanks. That was amazing, but rich."

She looked like she wanted to say something, but seemed to be hesitating.

"What?" he asked.

"You don't have to say, if you'd rather not. But I'd like to know why you *did* cancel out on me for prom. I appreciate your apology, and I promise I'm long over it. But I did always wonder."

Old resentments and shame tried to surface, but he refused to acknowledge them. He'd grown past those feelings. Hadn't he? He swallowed hard, but answered before he could think about it more.

"My mother was an alcoholic." Why was that so hard to say?

Her mouth opened into a little O, but she didn't say anything.

"She went on a bender that afternoon and was totally useless. Passed out and useless." He pulled in a deep breath. "Alyssa got her period. Freaked out. It hadn't occurred to me to check that my mother had told her about those things. I just assumed she knew. She was twelve."

He got up and pulled a Coke out of the fridge, pointed it at Rose. She shook her head so he shut the fridge and sat back down, opening the can. He took a drink and continued.

"Once I got her calmed down, and she realized she wasn't dying, she knew what it was. Her friends had talked some. But she was still upset, and she was royally pissed at Mom. Later, when she remembered it was prom night, she was mad at me for canceling but I just..." He ran a hand over his hair, rubbed at his neck. "I needed to be there for her."

Finally meeting her gaze, he shrugged. "Maybe it didn't matter in the long run, but it was important to her that day. And me."

"Ethan, of course it was. You made the right decision."

He shook his head. "It's not…when the choice is between hurting one person or another, it sucks."

"Yeah, it does. But you made the right one that day."

"Thanks. It means a lot that you think so. It got old fast, disappointing people, so I found it's better to not make a commitment in the first place. Not when I never knew if my mother's actions would screw up my plans."

"I'm sorry. I had no idea about your mom. That's really shitty, and I hate that you were struggling with it and I didn't know. I remember when you missed the start of the homecoming game, that same year. You said your mom fell and was in the hospital."

"Yeah. Man, coach was pissed. He didn't want to let me play, but he also hated to lose. When I finally got him calmed down enough to tell him I'd been at the hospital, that she'd broken her wrist, he was better."

"I wish you hadn't felt like you needed to keep that all a secret." She reached out and put her hand on his arm.

It was ridiculous to feel choked up about it, all these years later. He supposed he should have gone to therapy or something.

"It's hard to know what to do at that age. I was ashamed and afraid if people found out, they would try and take us from mom, which would probably mean being separated from Alyssa." He took a long pull of his soda, cooling his throat. "You know Mrs. Taylor, the librarian? At the town library, not the school."

"Yes, she's my mom's best friend."

He nodded. "That's right, I forgot that. She pulled me aside one day. I know she was trying to be helpful. Give advice more than criticize." He shook his head, no longer sure he wanted to share this. His gut had tightened and he pulled in a breath.

Rose moved her chair closer to his and took his hand between both of hers. Her warmth seeped through when he hadn't thought he was cold.

"Things hadn't been as bad before that year. That's why I had planned on going to college. I was so excited when I got the scholarship. Now that I think about it, maybe that's why she started drinking more. Realizing she wasn't going to be able to handle it if I left. I guess it's my fault she got worse, which then meant there was no way I could leave Alyssa there, alone with her."

He was startled when Rose jerked her hands free, but she immediately put them on either side of his face. Her expression was fierce, uncompromising.

"Don't you dare say that. Or feel that. I know I can't tell you what to feel, but fuck that, I am. Don't you dare feel like it was your fault she did that. *None* of it was your fault."

He blinked, staring into her eyes, which were damp. Taking in a deep breath, he nodded, her hands moving along with his head.

"I know. Usually I know. Sometimes I fall back to that place in my head, but usually I know."

She scowled at him for a moment, searching his face, then let go and sat back. "Okay. What did that have to do with Belinda Taylor?"

She took his hand back into her possession, resting them on her thigh.

"Um. Right. I think it was sometime shortly after that homecoming game, actually. She took me aside and said I needed to try to do better. As we were two of the few Black families in town, our reputations had to be better than the rest of town. Otherwise it would become too easy for the white folks to start to judge and look down on us."

Rose stared at him, her brow furrowed. "Seriously?"

"Yeah. She said people thought I was lazy and disrespectful when I didn't show up somewhere I was supposed to, and that it wouldn't be long before that impression I gave turned into something more."

"Wow. I don't know what to say about that. I don't know what to *think* about it."

"I wasn't thrilled to be having the conversation, that's for sure. I had never really thought about my being Black like that. I sort of get where she was coming from, what she was trying to do. But it was a shock to me."

"You didn't tell her about your mom. And you decided if people didn't expect you to be somewhere, they couldn't be disappointed when you weren't."

"Basically. It was easier after I graduated and had more control over what I was expected to do and where and when."

He tried to pull his hand back, suddenly feeling foolish for the entire conversation, but she somehow misinterpreted the gesture and ended up leaning in and hugging him.

The lump in his throat reappeared. She tugged him up to standing so she could move in and hold him tight. Wrapping his arms around her, he just soaked her in.

CHAPTER SIX

Rose breathed in the scent of Ethan, trying to calm the tingling in her nose that threatened to turn into tears. To know that he had been going through these things back then, and she'd had no clue, was heartbreaking.

He gave an extra squeeze of his arms, and it suddenly hit her that she was hugging Ethan. She could feel the muscles under her hands, the easy strength of a man who spent his time working with his hands and body instead of at a computer. He was taller than her by about five inches, which suddenly seemed to be just about the perfect height.

Abruptly, she pulled away, sitting back down in the chair. She balled up the cupcake wrapper and napkin, willing her blush to recede. When she looked up, Ethan appeared to be fighting off a smile, but she gave him credit for the effort. His warm brown eyes showed amusement, but also a hint of interest. *Oh boy*.

"Want something to drink now? Water? Tea? Wine?"

She pulled her brain away from those kinds of thoughts and grasped at his offer. "Tea would be great, thanks."

She watched as he pulled an electric kettle from the back of the counter, filled it with water and switched it on. He reached up for a mug and tea bags and she enjoyed watching his body move. Liked the way he kept his hair cropped close to his scalp, inviting her to rub her hands over it and feel the texture.

Oh crap. She turned her attention back to the balled-up trash in her hands and found she'd squeezed it into a pulp.

It had been some time since she'd been so physically attracted to a man. The last couple of guys she'd "dated" mostly because they were convenient and on the same wavelength as her regarding prioritizing their work life over their relationships. Not that there'd been anything wrong with them, she just hadn't ever gotten hot and bothered watching them make a cup of tea.

Said cup slid in front of her as she stared at the tabletop.

"Are you okay?" Ethan asked. "I'm sorry if that was all too much for a random afternoon, with a mostly stranger."

"Oh, no! I'm glad you shared that with me. Really. And we're not strangers. I know it's been years, but you don't feel like a stranger to me. We spent just as many years knowing each other as I did away."

"Okay. Do you want milk or sugar? And are you going to tell me what had you so quiet?"

"Yes and yes, please. And…I don't know. It was kind of inappropriate."

"Oh, now I'm intrigued."

"Come on, you know you're a good-looking guy. I know you don't want for attention."

"Want for attention? Are you turning into your mother?"

She slapped her hands over her face. "Ah! Am I? Help me!"

His fingers encircled her wrists and pulled her hands away. She opened her eyes to find his only inches away. He was grinning, but as they stared at each other, the grin slipped away and her breathing picked up.

Slowly, very slowly, he closed the distance between them. Her eyes drifted shut one second before his lips met hers. Soft and warm and sweet. She enjoyed the sensation and considered opening her lips to get more, but he pulled back.

Opening her eyes again, she wasn't sure if she should say something. Do something.

"I wanted to do that a long time ago."

She smiled. "I wanted you to do that a long time ago."

He moved back in and this time teased her lips with his tongue until she opened for him, accepted him. Still gentle, still sweet, and yet her blood started to fire and her heart beat faster. He explored her, and she enjoyed every moment of it. When he retreated, she opened her eyes again, found he hadn't gone far.

"I wanted to do *that* since the night at Wolfhound."

"I wanted you to do that since the night at Wolfhound."

He was kneeling at the side of her chair, and she was twisted around to face him. She scooted so she was sideways on the chair, and he moved in between her knees. His long fingers speared into her hair and he kissed her again. But this time, it wasn't slow and it wasn't sweet. It was fierce, with dueling teeth and tongue, and she lost herself in it for what felt like forever, but it was over too soon when she pulled back with a gasp.

His fingers slid free of her hair, tracing along her cheekbones and her swollen lips, before dropping down to her thighs as he sat back on his heels.

"Wow. Well," she said.

"Well?"

"Maybe, if you think you might want to do that again, we should talk options."

"I would definitely like to do that again," he said. "Let's move to the couch."

She smirked. "That might be dangerous."

"Depends on your definition of dangerous."

She laughed and stood, pushing her chair back. Offering him one hand, she used the other to get her tea and moved into the living room.

It was decorated in what she considered late bachelor. Not the cast-offs of early bachelorhood, but not the more polished scheme of a man who'd decorated with a woman. Or a man who cared to put a room together with actual thought and attention. The couch didn't have any throw pillows, but was cushy. And it was dark blue. She gave him points for not going with black or brown leather. There was a generous ottoman positioned as a coffee table, with two remotes and an afghan laying on it. One side of the sofa had a floor lamp, and the other a side table, which held only a little bit of clutter.

A large-screen TV sat on a stand against the wall, with a narrow bookcase next to it. That pretty much covered the whole room.

She sat down and he offered her the afghan. Accepting it, she put her tea on the side table and sat so that she was mostly facing him when he took a seat in the middle of the couch.

Spreading the blanket out so that it covered them both, she just went ahead and threw it out there. "We just discussed how neither of us is ready for a relationship. Although, to be fair to you and totally honest, I think you should give some thought to how you're not in the same place you were when you made those decisions. Finding the right partner would be a support to you. It wouldn't need to be about competing priorities."

"But not you," he said.

"Right. What I said still holds. I don't even know where I'll be in eight months."

"Let's set the whole kissing thing aside for a minute. Tell me about that. About what it is that you're trying to do with you and your business."

"Okay, but I can get a little bit passionate about the subject, so stop me if I start to babble."

He laughed. "I promise."

"I'm a computer programmer. My specialty is to work with companies who have old software systems that are no longer getting the job done. I work with them to see if I can revamp what they have, bring it up to date, to solve current and future needs, or help them transition to a new system."

"Okay, sounds good so far."

"My plan has been to get my business to the stage that I can support myself, while still saving for retirement. I'm lucky that I only really need an internet connection to be in business, so I may not be able to support myself in an expensive city like Los Angeles, but I can here. Or in some small town in Japan, Spain or Thailand. Or wherever, as long as there's good internet and I find a lower cost of living area. My clients sometimes need in person meetings, but we've really transitioned to video chats to get things started and then mostly email to progress with the project."

"Have you traveled a lot?"

"No. So it's entirely possible I might not like living in any of those places, but the beauty of it is that I don't have to commit to any of them long term. I can keep trying new places, even here in the states, as long as it's not an expensive city. It's the freedom to move around wherever I want and however I want that sounds awesome. And yet, I'm sure I'll find a place that's home and settle eventually, but I'm hoping by then my income will be enough to support my having a home base and still be able to afford travel. And even then, I don't think I want to buy a home. I'd rather keep my options open."

"That's an awesome plan and an excellent goal. Sounds like you've put a lot of thought into it."

"My girlfriends and I had a sort of epiphany. And we realized we didn't want to get stuck in the office-work, nine-to-five grind that we were heading towards. And we didn't want to be stuck in the paycheck-to-paycheck lifestyle that we, and all of our friends, seemed to be in."

"Sounds like there's a story there."

She reached around and grabbed her tea, taking a nice long drink, since it had cooled. "Naomi and I have been friends since freshman year of college. We stole Janelle the next year, when one of our guy friends broke up with her and we decided to keep *her*, instead."

"Ha, nice."

"Anyway, the three of us became the closest, but we were part of a larger extended group. Which did include Janelle's ex. And our friend Leslie. It all started when Leslie moved in with her boyfriend."

"I'm sensing that didn't go well."

"Nope. They broke up eight months later, and she was screwed. She'd gotten a good job, decent salary, and was paying him half the rent, but was living paycheck to paycheck, and couldn't come up with a deposit on an apartment of her own, let alone buy any furniture."

She finished her tea and reached around to put it back on the table. "The three of us got to talking about it. How awful it was that she was a college graduate with a good job, and yet had no money saved and a mountain of student loan debt. The worst was that we all admitted to being in similar positions. Naomi had just bought her condo, and was renting out the second bedroom so she could afford her mortgage. Janelle was living with two roommates, and I had just gotten my own apartment. I'd still been living with my college roommates, and was proud of myself for saving enough to get my own place, but that wiped out my savings and my rent was taking about forty percent of my pay. And we all had decent jobs."

"The story of our times, right?"

She grimaced. "Exactly. I started fooling around online, looking into things. I found a personal finance community, and then a financial independence community. People dedicated to living below their means, instead of on credit, and saving enough to either retire very early or, more often, to have the freedom to only work when or if they wanted. Which means they only need to work the jobs they love, which makes it hardly like work at all."

"Get out of the nine-to-five grind you mentioned."

"Exactly."

"I can't claim to have done it intentionally, but at some point it did occur to me that I wouldn't have been happy in a white-collar office environment. I much prefer the freedom to go where I want to go and do what I want to do, as long as I get what needs to get done, done. Mostly, like I said earlier, I didn't want people expecting me on their timeline, but it worked out for me in the end."

"You're one of the lucky ones who found something you enjoy doing, and that, hopefully, pays enough to let you build for your future. People make fun of our generation, but I swear most of us are working harder than the oldies. It just doesn't look the same to them, so they scoff."

"And yet, they would be impressed you can use the word scoff without irony."

She laughed. "Maybe I was being ironic."

"Sure, let's go with that." He watched her for a minute. "I like that you have a plan. Goals. It's easy to get stuck in a rut. Or, like you said, the grind."

"What about you?"

His inhale was sharp. "I thought I would leave Wildlife Ridge behind. Only come back to visit and gloat about my success. I thought football would lead me to college, and I didn't know where that would lead, but I was sure it would be somewhere great."

"But you didn't leave, because of your mom."

"Because of my sister."

She nodded, feeling that in her gut. She was an only child, but it was easy to see, to remember, how important his sister was to him. He'd given up his whole future for her.

"No, don't get that look. Things have worked out well for me. I love it here. Like I said, I have a great situation, get to do what I want, when I want. I have the flexibility to help people out if I want to, like Mr. Houston, without committing to something that's going to get screwed up if I can't make it."

"That's something you still worry about? Even with your mom gone? I'm sorry about that, by the way. Even though she was a problem for you, I'm sure that was extremely difficult."

"I got your flowers when she passed. I appreciated them. It was hard, yeah. The sense of relief was awful, but huge."

"I bet."

"But by then, I was set up managing this building, and Alyssa was in college. I enjoy being part of the town. I have family, good friends and lots of acquaintances who've known me since birth. I still go to the high school football games and sometimes I go into Denver and have a little fun."

"Ooh, I think you should tell me more about that."

"I think you should come over here."

"Where? I'm right here."

"Closer."

"I think that could be dangerous," she repeated

"Define dangerous."

She laughed, charmed by his playful side. "Didn't we discuss staying friends? Me leaving town? You having commitment issues?"

"Didn't we discuss friends with benefits?" he asked.

"Yes. And I've done that in the past. Successfully. But that was in Los Angeles. Seems like a small town isn't conducive to that kind of thing. People would talk."

"And that bothers you?"

"I probably wouldn't be around to hear it. But you would be."

"I think I could handle it."

"I would hate for you to regret anything we did."

"I wouldn't. They'd probably relax. I think they're starting to wonder if I'm gay. Not that they'd have a problem with that. They'd probably finally move forward with the gay pride parade they've been thinking about since Jin and Cal moved in and opened the antique store. It's the not knowing that's killing them."

"Well. If you're sure, what are you doing way over there?"

She barely got the sentence out before he was much, much closer. His finger was under her chin, tipping her up so he could bring his lips down.

ETHAN FELT like it had been hours, days, since he'd kissed her, and finally, he could do it again. He rubbed his lips over hers, teasing when she tried to chase him down, then darting his tongue in to meet hers. She opened for him, hot and eager, and oh so sweet.

Her warm fingers drifted under his sweatshirt, snaking under to find his flesh. He tightened his muscles against the feel of her soft explorations. Taking it as a cue, he did some exploring of his own.

He had just moved his hands to her side, his thumbs brushing the undersides of her generous breasts, when his phone rang.

Damn. He had to let her go and check. It could be his sister or his brother-in-law. Or an emergency in the building. He opened his eyes, afraid to see disappointment or even condemnation in her gaze, but he found amused resignation instead.

It was actually a good interruption, because he was supposed to go to his sister's house for dinner. He knew he should tell Rose about Alyssa, in case she hadn't heard yet. She likely would have mentioned it if she had. But they'd already been so serious and dark today, he didn't want to bring it up. He glanced at the screen before answering.

"Hi, Mrs. Rubinski. How are you today?"

The conversation was fairly quick, with him promising to come down and fix her television within the hour. When he hung up, he rolled his eyes at Rose.

"She messes up the settings with the remote. I fix it. She does it again. Rinse and repeat. But she gives good cookies." He sighed. "I'm sorry."

She pursed her lips. "I don't know. It's probably good to slow things down a bit. You should be sure you're okay with what we talked about."

"I'm sure that I want to taste you more. And get my hands on your curves. And feel your fingers on more than just my abdomen."

She licked her lips.

He groaned.

Laughing, she stood up. "Good. I'm glad. Anna, up in apartment 310? She's coming over for dinner after her last yoga class, and then we're going to the Tavern. If you feel like heading that way, we could spend some time together. But no pressure, if you're involved in something else."

She was too good to be true. For a second, he tried to find the trap in the statement, figure out if she really meant it. Then he realized he was being unfair to her, and he had no reason not to take her at her word.

"Are you the woman of my dreams?" he asked, pleased when she laughed. He went into the kitchen and got her groceries out of the refrigerator. "I'll walk you to your apartment."

"You don't have to."

"Nope. But I want to. What are you making for dinner?"

"Pork chops, rice pilaf and spinach salad."

"I'd feel left out but I'm having dinner at my sister's house. I'll probably come by the bar, after, though. That would be nice. Is Anna's boyfriend out of town?"

"She has a boyfriend?"

He laughed. "Yes, and when he's home she's a homebody. But when he's gone, she becomes social."

"I'm taking a yoga class with her, but that hasn't given us much of a chance to get to know each other, which is why an evening out seemed perfect."

"She's great, she just likes to stay home with Doug when he's home. His business takes him out of town once a month or so."

They made it to her apartment and she unlocked the door. He handed her the bags then swooped in for a kiss, keeping it quick and light so he wouldn't be tempted to push her into the apartment and forget about where he was supposed to be going.

"Thanks," she said, breathlessly, when he stood back.

"You're welcome."

She laughed. "I meant thanks for carrying my bags."

"I know."

The door shut in his face, but he could hear her still laughing. With a grin of his own, he headed for Mrs. Rubinski's.

He had the television sorted quickly, then left, cookie in hand, to check on apartment 106's plumbing. The tenants had just moved out and reported a drip in the faucet. He was irritated they hadn't mentioned it before, and was pretty sure he'd gotten it fixed, but wanted to double check before he started the work on turning over the apartment the next day.

A quick check proved everything was in order, so he headed out to his sister's house.

As soon as Jackson opened the door, Ethan knew it hadn't been a good day for Alyssa. Jackson just nodded as he let Ethan in, and Ethan took in a deep breath, then pasted a smile on his face.

CHAPTER SEVEN

When he pulled up to Wolfhound Tavern, Ethan turned off the truck then sat, hands on the wheel, staring blankly through the windshield. Alyssa had been throwing up most of the day and had looked drawn and pale. Her spirits were low, though she'd tried to buck up for him, as she always did. Which unfailingly nearly killed him to see. She was the one suffering, but she was always convinced that she was making things worse for *him*.

For fuck's sake, she was miserable and in pain and she didn't want him to be upset? His hands tightened on the wheel and he closed his eyes, tight enough to see sparks.

It was probably a bad idea to go into the bar. He wasn't in a cheerful mood and he didn't want to inflict that on Rose. Or anyone. But he also didn't want to go home and stare at the television, either. He didn't want to go home alone.

Maybe he should get a dog. But then, he didn't want another living being dependent on him for food and bathroom breaks and exercise. Love wasn't the issue. He knew he could give a dog plenty of that, and soak up what the dog had to give. But it took a lot more than that to keep a dog happy and healthy.

For crying out loud, how he'd gone from thinking about his sister to thinking he'd be a failure as a dog owner, he didn't know, but it wasn't helping the situation, that was for sure. Before he could think about it much more, he opened the door and got out. And realized he'd walked right out of his sister's house without his coat. Damn, he really had been out of it.

He hustled inside so he could warm up. Luckily it wasn't snowing or raining. The blast of heat was welcoming, but even more so was the noise of people and activity. Healthy people, and healthy activity. Once in a while someone got obnoxiously drunk at the Tavern, and gave him bad memories of his mom, but that was rare. He usually made a quick exit in those instances and was fine.

He rubbed his hands together and blew on them, moving towards the bar. Sandra was running the taps and he held up a finger for one, pointing towards the left so she'd know he wanted the Uncle Henry's. He veered off to a table with several people hanging around it, including Rose and Anna. Rose spotted him first, her automatic smile warming him up further.

She jumped up and gave him a hug.

"Holy crap, you're freezing!" She ran her hands up and down his arms.

"I'll warm up in a minute. You guys have a good dinner?" He dragged a stool over between her and Ian, who made more room for him.

"Mr. Fix It! Glad you came out. You need me to flag down a server?"

"Nah, Sandra's got me covered." He greeted the others at the table. Jin and Cal, and Tom Romano, the mayor's husband, who worked at Skunk's gas station and was one of the town's biggest gossips.

Rose and Anna were obviously feeling good and a bit tipsy, though not in a way that concerned him. In fact, he felt a bit of the weight of the evening slide off his shoulders as he saw their easy smiles. Rose was scooping a healthy bite of spinach artichoke dip onto a tortilla chip, her eyes alive with pleasure.

Ian nudged a plate of stuffed mushroom caps his way, and he considered it. He hadn't eaten much at dinner. At the time, it had felt like he'd never want food again. And he wasn't quite there yet now, but maybe after a bit of the drink one of the servers was dropping off.

He took a sip of the hard apple cider and tuned into the conversation that had resumed around him. They seemed to be debating the merits of a particular type of seasoning packet. He found he just couldn't bring himself to relate at that moment, so he soaked it all in without really paying much attention.

Rose's hand rested on his shoulder, and she leaned in close to his ear. The music was normal bar volume, so they'd been shouting at each other across the table. Her breath whispered against his ear.

"Are you okay?"

He nodded, offered a bit of a smile.

"Would you rather leave? I can go with you."

He shook his head, leaned in towards her ear. "I'm not feeling super talkative, but I'd rather stay and enjoy the atmosphere."

She searched his face for a minute, then nodded. Reaching past him, she picked up one of the mushrooms and offered it to him, holding it close to his lips. Held between her delicate fingers, the morsel suddenly appeared much more appetizing to him than it had a few minutes ago. He opened his mouth and took it from her, his gaze on hers the whole time.

When he licked his lips, he was pretty sure her eyes dilated. He smiled, and this time it was much more genuine.

From the corner of his eye he saw Cal waggle his eyebrows and Anna looked like she was going to say something, but Jin bumped her shoulder.

The music changed to a western song and Jin grabbed Anna and swung her out to a clear area near the tables. Rose shimmied in her seat, but made no move to go dance. Tom was telling Ian about his grandmother's secret manicotti ingredient, and Ethan made a mental note to ask Ian about it later, but he didn't want to interrupt right now. Rose put her hand back on his shoulder, and he turned to her, but she was just listening to Cal.

Anna and Jin returned and the conversation flowed to a movie they were interested in seeing. Apparently it was something Cal and Anna were sure the others would love, though Rose, Jin and Ian were skeptical. Without actually saying anything, Ethan found himself included in the plans to drive out to Bell View.

He considered commenting about trying to make it but not being sure if he could, but he decided that with the group scenario, if he had to back out at the last minute, it wouldn't be a problem.

It was nice, sitting there and being quiet, and yet unquestionably being included in the group conversation. When the waiter stopped by to check on them, Ian said he needed to get going, and Jin and Cal stood. Anna and Rose gathered up their purses as Tom moved off to one of the pool tables. Ethan had only drunk half his cider, but he was okay with that.

He had a feeling Rose would lose her mind if he tried to walk out of the bar without a jacket, so he told them he was going to the bar to pay his tab, and said his goodbyes. Feeling more himself by the time he made it to the bar, he let Sandra and Shirley, the town's mayor, drag him into a conversation about the distinction between the stout and the Irish ale on tap, before finally heading out.

Jumping into his truck, he cranked up the heat, even knowing it would only just be getting going by the time he got home, but at least that way he'd have a blast of warmth before making the dash from the truck to the building. He checked his phone to be sure he hadn't missed any messages from Alyssa or Jackson, then sent a quick one himself. Jackson responded to say that Alyssa was resting and not to worry. Yeah, well, that was impossible, but for now he could let it go.

He scanned the lot at the apartment, making sure everything was okay. Mrs. Rubinski's car could use an ice scraper, but he'd do that in the morning. With everything as right in his world as he was capable of making it for that day, he jogged inside.

Rose worked hard on Thursday. She had a challenging assignment that she was enjoying, though the client was...difficult. Particular, she could say. Her phone alerted her to the fact that she needed to get out of her office chair now if she wanted to make it to her yoga class on time. She groaned, stretching. As much as she'd like to keep working, her body was certain the yoga class was the smarter move. She'd been sitting for eight hours, only getting up for brief breaks.

Knowing she'd be ending the workday with the class, she'd given herself permission to wear her yoga clothes all day, so she was all ready to go.

She opened the door to find Ethan and her next-door neighbor walking towards her. Ethan was carrying what appeared to be about ten cloth grocery bags, while Claudia held a potted plant and her keys. Damn, she had never realized how sexy a helpful man was to her. Of course, it didn't hurt that he was sexy altogether, but her heart did a little melty thing at what she saw.

She gave them a quick greeting, waiting until Claudia's attention was on her door before giving Ethan a look that, hopefully, said they would be resuming their sexy times soon, then headed out.

Yoga had never been her thing in Los Angeles, but after meeting Anna at the apartment building, she'd decided to give it a go. She was spending a lot of hours on the computer, so her body could use the stretching and the workout, for sure. Plus, it got her out of the house and talking to people, which she was discovering she needed now that she'd stopped going into an office every day. She'd also signed up for a cookie decorating class at the bakery and gone to a book reading at the library.

Although she didn't know if she intended to stay in Wildlife Ridge long term, she was determined to be a part of the community no matter where she was residing. So far, it had been working out well for her, and she'd enjoyed meeting new people in a way she'd seemed to have lost over the years.

She swung into Lavender and Mint, the pharmacy, as she passed, hoping they'd have a headband she could buy. The little bell on the door tinkled cheerily.

"I'll be right with you," a woman's voice called out.

"No hurry," Rose answered, glancing down the aisles, hoping to see something relevant. The pharmacy sported an old-fashioned soda counter, and had enough old-school charm to be fun, but was still modern and practical enough that she had high hopes for finding what she'd come for.

"Rose! I'd heard you were back in town."

She turned to see a familiar face, a classmate who she was friends with on social media. She was a little on the short side, sporting a blonde bob which fit her face perfectly, and her smile of greeting had Rose going in for a hug.

"Erin, I was going to see if you wanted to meet up for dinner one of these days, after I get settled a little bit."

"I know you just got to town a couple of weeks ago, and I also know you've had time to have evenings out with Ethan, twice."

She said it with enough of a laughing tease that Rose knew she wasn't irritated.

"Wow, seriously?" Rose asked. "I mean, the first night I was at the bar with my dad and friend, and the second night there was a whole group of us!"

Erin laughed. "Oh honey, you're the hot topic right now, you have to know that."

Rose sighed and shook her head, amused. "Fine. I get it. Anna's convinced me to take a yoga class today. I need a headband or something, can you hook me up?"

Erin led her to the correct aisle. "How are things going with you? You posted something about working from home now?"

"Yes, I'm doing programming. It's great, I love it. You went back east for school, right?"

"Chicago, actually. Got my pharmacy degree and got married. We moved here just after we had our baby, and stayed, even though the marriage didn't last long."

"I'm sorry to hear that." Rose handed over her credit card as they talked and tried on the headband, using the window as a mirror. Someone waved to her, but she couldn't tell who it was, so she just waved back.

"Do you have time to sit for a minute? We can go to the soda counter."

"Sure, but I'll just have water. Seems wrong to begin my yoga journey with soda, even if it is deliciously flavored."

She settled onto a stool as Erin fussed around, handing her a glass of water with a slice of lemon. "It sucked that the marriage didn't work out, but I have my daughter, Olivia. Livvy. She's four now, and I have no regrets about having her in my life, so I can't complain. I'm sure you'll hear about it, since Bob, my ex, still lives here. He cheated on me with our next-door neighbor."

Erin came back around the counter with a mug of hot tea for herself and sat down.

"What an ass," Rose said.

"You remember Mike Harmon from our year? His younger brother, Josh, lives in the house next door. He was married to Patty and has two kids, one younger than Livvy, one older. His Patty and my Bob started it up together about six months after we moved in."

"Wow. That sucks. Did she pretend to be your friend, too?"

Erin blew on her tea. "Thankfully, no, she wasn't that awful. I mean, we were friendly, neighborly, but nothing more. Poor Josh, though, his daughter was only six months old when we moved in. He's a teacher at the elementary school."

Rose took a drink, wondering if she was hearing something in the other woman's voice or just imagining it. "Is that right?"

"He's a great guy. Great teacher. The kids love him. The community was pretty harsh on Patty, to be honest. Not that she didn't deserve it, but he had to put the word out to get people to stop talking badly about her, seeing as how she's his children's mother."

"Sounds like a stand-up guy. Were people harsh on Bob, too?"

"Yes, but not as much, since we'd only just moved to town. You remember how small-town life is, you have to take the bad to get the good. I'm actually surprised she's stuck around, but she's a fairly decent mother, and I think people are taking Josh's lead of being polite to her now."

Rose was finding that she did remember how small-town life was. She'd witnessed hundreds of conversations just like this between her mother and whomever she'd stopped to chat with in the store or on the street. If that person had a kid, too, Rose would hang out with them while the mothers talked. If not, she was expected to keep herself entertained for a few minutes while they caught up. Now, here she was, the one doing the catching up. It was surreal, but not in a bad way. She wondered how many conversations just like this had happened about her over the years. Thankfully, she'd done nothing she minded folks gabbing good naturedly about.

"Are they still together? Bob and Patty?"

"No, they broke up as soon as I caught them. Bob bought a house over on Glaring Road and he's fixing it up to turn it into a B&B. He's got family money and was managing a hotel in the city, but decided he didn't like the commute. It works out, we split custody fifty-fifty. I'd rather have her full time, of course, but she loves her daddy, so I'm glad he didn't decide to move to another area."

"Sounds like you're all making the best of the situation. Tell me more about Josh. Is he hot? Because it kind of sounds like he's hot." She grinned as the blush crept over Erin's face.

"I said he's a good dad and a good teacher!"

"Yeah, you did. And I remember that Mike was a pretty good-looking guy in high school, so maybe his brother is a pretty good-looking guy in his thirties?"

Erin began to toy with the necklace she was wearing. "He's handsome."

"Uh huh."

Erin laughed with her. "He's handsome, he's been a good neighbor, and that's it. We went through a bad experience, sort of together, that's all there is to it."

"Why?"

"Why what?"

"Why is that all there is to it? How long has it been since the divorce?"

"Two years."

"And is he dating? Are you?"

"Who has time to date when you're a working single parent?"

"Mm hm. Just asking the question. How come I've been here for twenty minutes and have yet to see a picture of your daughter?"

"Oh, I'll show you pictures, but don't think you've changed the subject quickly enough that I'll forget to ask you more details about these nights out with Ethan Woodford. I guess you've forgiven him for making you miss the prom?"

Rose waved that away as she scrolled through pictures on Erin's phone. "Oh, I can't with this level of cuteness!" She put her hand on her heart at the picture of the little girl dressed as a fairy for Halloween.

"Right. Now, back to Ethan."

"What? Ethan is Ethan. Like I already told you, I was with other people at the bar. Both times. Perfectly innocent."

Erin raised her eyebrows at her. "Perfectly innocent. Sure, I'll let you get away with that until we can sit down for that dinner and then we can discuss the innocent consumption of mushrooms being fed by hand."

Rose busted out laughing. Wow, people were definitely talking. She hoped Ethan was as okay with that as he'd indicated. "Fine, as long as you remember that interrogations go both ways." Rose sighed and slipped off the stool and they hugged.

THE CLASS WAS enjoyable and Rose figured she'd give it another try. She'd worried she'd feel slow and stupid since it wasn't a class just for beginner's but Anna had made her feel completely comfortable.

She *was* feeling a little bit sweaty afterward, but Anna and one of the older gentlemen in the class convinced her to walk over with them for coffee.

"Okay, but don't let me get anything from the bakery," she agreed.

"No promises," Anna said, grabbing her arm so she couldn't back out.

Laughing, Rose wondered how many calories she'd actually burned during the class. Probably not enough to justify a pastry, but oh well. They moved slowly as Ben had a cane.

"Doc says I need to keep using this for another week," he grumbled.

"You're doing awesome. Doc originally told you it would be a lot longer."

"He always underestimates us retirees."

"I think he assumes very few people will actually do the rehabilitation exercises he gives them, let alone continue attending their yoga classes, so he tacks on extra time to account for that."

Ben grunted as he held the door open for them. "Maybe," he conceded.

"I'm assuming you guys don't mean Doctor Peters, since she was a woman," Rose said, since when she'd been a kid, the woman had also been referred to as 'Doc'".

"Nope, her son, Kyle, took over a few years back. They worked together for a while, then she retired. We just called them both Doc. Still do, come to that. Just because she doesn't poke and prod at me anymore, doesn't mean I'm going to start calling her Helen."

He said this as if there may have been an argument about exactly that. Rose and Anna gave each other quick looks, but decided not to pursue the issue.

When they'd gotten their mochas and lattes and muffins, they found a small table near the fireplace.

"What happened, Ben? Did you have an accident?" Rose asked, blowing on her drink.

"Yes, well. I slipped on my walkway. It had started to buckle, and there was snow so I didn't see it. I tripped and turned my damn ankle."

"Ouch. I'm sorry, that must have been painful and annoying."

"The annoying part was the worst."

She laughed. "I bet."

"I'm not ashamed to admit that I was glad when Ethan came by to fix the path. I don't know how long it would have taken me to get to it, and I didn't like to think someone else coming to visit me could trip as well. Or even Donna. She walks that path every day to deliver the mail, and I would hate to see her take a fall."

"Mr. Fix It? Why am I not at all surprised," Anna said, spooning up a bit of the whipped cream from her drink.

"Yes, the afternoon when I came home from the hospital, he had the path mostly torn up by the time I got there, and asked me what I wanted laid in its place. Had a couple of options ready for me to see." He took a small sip of his mocha. "If I were a younger man, I might have been foolish enough to be insulted. But this old man was thankful. He had it all finished by dinnertime. My neighbor brought over a casserole and he dished some up for us and we were good to go."

"Aww, that is so sweet," Anna said. "He's a good guy." She eyed Rose over her drink. "You guys seemed fairly cozy at the bar. Anything going on there?"

"Hmm. I guess we'll have to see. I think he's coming with us all to the movie on Friday."

"You could certainly do worse than that guy, if you plan on staying in Wildlife Ridge. I have a hard time imagining him living somewhere else," Ben said.

"Well, being neighbors and going to the movies with a group of people is a long way from wondering what city someone wants to live in forever," Rose said, trying to keep the amusement out of her voice.

"You young people today seem to move either too fast or too slow. He's a good guy, no reason not to jump on that if you think you'll stick around. He deserves some good in his life."

Rose nearly spit out the sip of coffee she'd just taken. "Jump on that?"

He flushed. "You know what I mean. Dating. Going steady."

"Mm hmm."

"He doesn't date people from town much," Anna mused. "I always assumed it was because he's a little on the private side and doesn't like everyone gossiping about this love life."

"Or maybe he just doesn't have one," Ben suggested.

Anna scoffed. "Um, have you seen him?"

Ben pretended to scowl at her. "Looks aren't everything. The boy was taking care of his mom. And now his sister. He deserves a good woman in his life."

Rose had been about to steer the conversation in another direction, but that stopped her. "Alyssa?"

Anna's face got sad and Rose's gut clenched.

"Yeah, she has cancer. Again."

"Beat the breast cancer about three years ago, but got sick again about four, five months back," Ben added.

"Oh, no." Rose felt physically sick at the news. She knew he'd gone to see Alyssa before coming to the bar the other night, and now his quiet demeanor there made more sense. Not that it had bothered her, she'd just sensed that he was off. Maybe she should have tried harder to draw him out. Though he had seemed better by the time they'd left, so maybe he'd known exactly what he'd needed to feel better.

"She's fighting it, though," Ben said. "She beat it once, and she can do it again. Her husband is there for her, and of course, Ethan. The town has done a couple of fundraisers to help out, and we organize meals for her every couple of weeks. Her best friend, Pam, makes sure that when they need casseroles and freezer meals, we get that handled. You don't know Pam, she moved here with her family after you left."

"Wow, that's so awful. She's so young."

"She'll beat it," Ben sort of repeated, his voice gruff.

Rose got the feeling he wanted to make it so, just with the power of his words. "Well, please let me know if I can help with the food. I make a pretty good freezer meal."

Checking her watch, Anna stood. "I need to head back. I have one more class before I call it done."

Rose bid them both goodbye and walked home slowly, her thoughts wrapped up in Ethan and Alyssa.

CHAPTER EIGHT

Ethan knew as soon as he saw Rose on Friday that she'd heard about his sister. He'd texted her an hour ago to let her know he'd meet her and Anna at her apartment, to join them for the movie night. Her eyes were suspiciously wet when she opened her door to him and gave him a tight hug.

"Oh, Ethan."

"Can we talk about it later?" he asked. He'd suspected she would hear about Alyssa sooner, rather than later. He probably should have told her himself. He knew they'd have to talk about it later, but it was a relief to him that she already knew. Maybe it had been cowardly of him to handle it this way. Probably. But...just saying the words hurt so *damn* much.

"Yeah, we can talk about it later. Let's go enjoy the movie." She frowned, and then seemed to shake it off, determined to have a good time. "I hope so anyway. It's not really my type of movie, but Cal and Anna were so enthusiastic about it."

"It's good to stretch yourself now and then. At the very least, if it sucks, that should give us some good ammunition against them for some fun teasing."

"True." She checked her watch. "Anna texted that she's on her way down. We can meet her halfway."

He felt absurdly grateful that she wasn't pushing him to talk about Alyssa. She locked up and led the way to the staircase. They made it halfway down the hall before the door opened and Anna bounced out.

"Awesome, you're ready. I was thinking we should grab sushi. That's one of the few foods we don't have a good option for here in town. If you guys side with me, we can overwhelm the opposition. If there is any," she added with a grin, before turning back around and bounding down the stairs.

"Shouldn't she be tired from working out all day?" Ethan asked.

When they made it to the foyer, Jin and Cal were sitting on the little bench Ethan had set up next to the mailboxes and Ian was walking through the front door.

"Dude! Ethan, are you actually coming? We got you off the internet long enough for a drive and a movie?" He directed a wide grin at Rose. "A pretty woman moves back to town and suddenly you're social again."

Jin and Cal, who had risen to meet them, just shook their heads at Ian. Anna was more direct, slapping him in the arm.

"Hey, I'm just teasing," Ian said, not sounding at all repentant. "I even brought the Durango so we'd all fit." He held the door open and gestured for them to proceed him.

"When I was in high school, we used to cram six people into a Honda Civic for this trip," Rose said.

"Exactly. This will be much more comfortable, I promise."

Rose climbed in first, making her way to the far back. She probably expected Anna to follow her, but it was Ethan who settled into the next seat. Her lips twitched, but she didn't say anything as Jin and Cal took the two middle seats and Anna claimed shotgun, already arguing her choice for dinner with Ian.

"Do you like sushi?" Rose asked quietly as Ian made a counterargument for his favorite build-your-own-burger joint.

"I do, yes."

"Can't you build your own burger at several places in town?" Jin asked.

"It's not the same," Ian argued as he pulled onto the highway. "This place has lots of extra options that a non-burger place doesn't have. Besides, they also don't serve raw fish."

"What about you, Cal?" Anna asked.

"I pushed for the movie choice, I'll go along with the majority on the dinner choice."

"Hey," Anna laughed. "No fair, the movie was my choice, too."

"Ha!" Ian said. "That's totally fair. What about you, Jin? Don't be a cliché."

"So, it would be cliché if a Japanese guy likes sushi?" Cal asked, incredulously.

"Well…sort of," Ian admitted, this time sounding chagrined.

"I love a good burger," Jin said.

Ian pumped his arm in victory.

"I had a fantastic one for lunch, as a matter of fact," Jin continued. "At the Taphouse."

Ian pretended to pout. At least, Ethan was fairly certain he was pretending. "Dude, if you wanted lunch and a beer, why didn't you come to the Tavern?"

"Because I wanted one of Fay's amazing burgers. If you ate there, you wouldn't think the place you mentioned going to tonight is all that."

The whole car laughed, and Anna changed the subject, apparently figuring that had won the debate on where they were eating dinner.

The conversation was easy as they made their way to the city. Ethan had confirmed that Jackson was home from work tonight, so he even managed to keep his phone in his pocket and not check it every ten minutes, in case he'd missed a text.

"Hey, Rose, have you talked to your friend Naomi since she left?" Ian asked.

"Of course."

"Did she mention me at all? When is she coming back for a visit?"

Rose laughed. "I can't say she did, sorry. And she'll be back soon."

"You sound like I don't have a chance."

"Well…"

"Aww, come on. I haven't been able to show her any of my moves yet, but I'm sure if I did…"

"Right. Well, you know, anything is possible."

Anna and Cal were laughing outright.

"What, do I need to be a YouTube star to catch her attention? Or, does she not date white guys?" Ian asked.

Ethan groaned and slapped his hand to his head in a way that told her he wished he could slap his friend's head.

"Sure she does," Rose answered. "She dates guys that are— Never mind. Go ahead and make a play for her."

"Nah, come on, you have to finish that sentence."

"Somehow I don't think you'd like the result of that," Ethan cautioned his friend, trying to keep his own laughter at bay. One thing Ian did not suffer from was a lack of confidence.

"Hey." Rose made her voice extra cheerful. "You know what I love at sushi places that isn't raw fish? Shrimp tempura. Are you a fan of shrimp?"

Jin was snickering now, but trying to hide it behind his hand.

Even Ian laughed. "Aw, come on. Tell me why she wouldn't be interested."

"What is your long-term plan? For supporting yourself."

Ian frowned, turning serious. "Everyone knows my uncle will most likely leave the bar to me. And it's a good, successful business."

"Right. It is. But you're just planning on treading water until it's handed to you. *Probably* handed to you."

"So, being a future business owner may or may not be okay, but being a bar manager isn't?"

Ethan knew Ian well enough to understand he wasn't upset, but Rose gave him a questioning look. Ethan nodded his head and jerked his chin towards the driver's seat, letting her know it was okay to continue, but she still seemed a little tense.

"She'd be fine with a bar manager, even a bartender, as long as he had plans and goals for the future. Plans that don't rely on inheritance."

"Yeah, well, considering my uncle is only like twenty years older than me, I might need to revisit some of my plans and goals."

Rose relaxed at Ian's cheerful response and Ethan reached over to squeeze her hand.

"What does your friend do?" Anna asked. "Maybe she'll move here, too, and Ian will have plenty of time to figure out how to fix his future and woo the girl."

"She's a landlord. Owns and manages a few properties."

"Stuck in Los Angeles, then, it sounds like."

"No, once she gets to a certain level, she'll hand the buildings over to management companies she trusts and run them remotely."

Ian put his hand to his heart. "There's still hope!"

"I don't know," Anna teased. "You'd have to convince her before she hears about the new guy in town."

Ian scoffed. "She'd have to see him first. And he never comes into town, does he? He sure hasn't been to the Tavern. Who moves to Wildlife Ridge and doesn't come into the Tavern? It's been a couple of months, hasn't it?"

"Who's this?" Rose asked.

"A guy bought the big place out on Toad Lane. Supposedly it's just him, no family. But no one in town seems to have met him, except the realtor, and he's playing coy," Cal answered. "And he only moved into the house about six weeks ago, remember? That's when the big moving truck went through town. The driver told Tom the owner's name was Aaron."

"But the word is he's on the younger side," Jin added. "Not some old dude."

"So everyone's assuming he's pretty wealthy. That house was listed for a million-five," Ian said.

"But it was listed for over a year," Anna added.

"That doesn't make sense," Ethan said. "Why would a single guy buy that big place? It has to have at least four bedrooms."

"Privacy," Cal said. "It's technically past the town limits. It's the biggest parcel of land, I bet. And there are gates at the end of the driveway."

"Hm, maybe so," Ethan acknowledged. He decided they'd done enough gossiping, though. "Are you two happy to no longer be the new guys in town?"

"Seriously!" Cal laughed. "I was so excited when I heard. But I don't think enough people even realize he's there, so they're still mostly treating us like the newbies. Shirley Romano stopped me as I was going into City Pizza to make sure I knew the semi-annual swap meet would be at the Masonic Temple banquet hall on the seventh. As if I haven't been here for two years. As if I don't get the newspaper."

"As if she thinks we sell swap meet finds at the antique store," Jin added.

"More like she's hoping we'll sell some stuff on the cheap," Cal laughed.

As Ian slowed to exit the freeway, Ethan realized he was still holding Rose's hand. He gave it a little squeeze and she turned to look at him.

He waggled his eyebrows. "Can we neck back here on the way home?" he asked in a whisper. Her quiet laughter pleased him.

ROSE SHIVERED when they walked out of the restaurant. She was feeling full and pleasantly buzzed as they'd shared a bottle of sake, but the wind had picked up. She took her knit cap out of her purse and pulled it on, bringing it down to cover the tips of her ears. She sniffled and checked her pocket, pleased to find the packet of tissues where it was supposed to be.

Ethan took her hand as they walked with the group across the street and down the block to the movie theater. The sidewalks had been cleared, so it was an easy stroll.

Despite his bitching, Ian had seemed to have no trouble finding plenty to eat and was in a cheerful mood now, teasing Cal and Jin about what they could sell at the upcoming swap meet.

She sneezed, and had to work to get a tissue free while wearing her gloves, but managed it.

"Bless you," Anna told her.

"Thanks. I think my nose might take the longest to get used to this weather."

"You haven't even gone the full winter," Cal teased. "What if you've turned into a Cali girl and can't stand it?"

"I'll move to Bora Bora," she said with a grin. "As long as they have internet, I'm good."

"Ooh," Anna breathed. "I was thinking the Virgin Islands."

They debated tropical locations while they got their tickets and found seats. She was way too full to consider a snack, but Anna, Cal and Ian went back for popcorn and sodas. She sniffled again and made a mental note to get another pack of tissues for her pocket before she ran out.

As the lights dimmed and Rose got comfortable in her seat, she had to resist the urge to get comfortable by leaning into Ethan's inviting heat. She kind of thought he'd be okay with it, but she was trying to keep in mind that they'd both been clear about what they were looking for. Not that friends with benefits weren't allowed to enjoy a movie together, but they'd barely gotten to the friends part of their relationship, and she didn't want to set false expectations. But also, he'd held her hand. Twice. Probably she was overthinking things, and she should just turn off her brain and enjoy the movie.

She tried. She did. But the movie was so boring she didn't come close to succeeding. Ethan shifted beside her, and she suspected he was as bored as she was. Anna, on her other side, also seemed a bit restless.

Finally, it was over. They all kept silent until they were back on the sidewalk.

"Sorry," Anna said.

"That was fantastic," Cal said.

"Dude," Ian said, shaking his head. "Seriously?"

"You don't get to pick for, like, the next five movies," Jin said, shaking his head.

"You guys are uncultured Neanderthals."

They teased him for part of the ride home, then discussed movies the rest of them actually liked until they pulled up in front of Salmon Springs. They said their good nights and she was slightly disappointed when Ethan headed towards his apartment, while she followed Anna to the stairs. She was tired, it had been a pleasant but long day, but sitting with him in the backseat for the whole ride home, she'd been wishing they could do some of that necking he'd mentioned.

She let herself into the apartment just as her phone buzzed. She smiled at seeing the text from Ethan, asking if he could come up for a minute.

Sending a quick yes, she turned on a lamp and checked to see that there wasn't any mess lying around. Other than the paperwork scattered around her desk it was in good shape. The plant he'd given her was on the side table and actually doing pretty well, so she didn't need to hide it in shame. She pulled off her cap and fluffed her hair. Wished she had time to go check a mirror.

Hearing his footsteps, she opened the door, welcoming him in with a smile.

He closed the door behind himself, threaded his fingers through her hair and kissed her.

It started out lazy and teasing, but before long, possibly because she moved her body into full contact with his, it became more demanding.

When she was having trouble breathing, he pulled free, his thumbs caressing her cheekbones as they stared at each other.

"I've been thinking about the taste of you for hours," he said.

"I was having indecent ideas about your skin, soy sauce and sake, over dinner," she told him.

He groaned and dove in for another kiss. The temptation to pull at his shirt, get her hands on his body was great, but she reminded herself that it was late, she had an early conference call scheduled, and when she first had him, she wanted to take her time. So she forced her hands to stay on his hips, her fingers digging into his jeans.

This time it was she who pulled back. He groaned and rested his forehead against hers as they both struggled for breath.

"Soon," he said.

She wasn't sure if it was a promise, a demand, or a plea, but she was fully onboard whichever it was.

"Soon," she agreed. "But not tonight."

He brushed his lips over hers, then stepped back.

"I'm making lasagna tomorrow. You're welcome to stop by if the timing works out for you."

She wasn't entirely sure what flashed across his face at that, but she suspected it was panic. Reaching out, she cupped his cheek. "I'm making it no matter what, and eating it no matter what. If you're there, too, great. If not, more leftovers for me. It's not a big deal, either way."

"It's not that I don't want to. I'm just not sure I can make it. I need to check on Alyssa, and run some errands—"

"Ethan," she interrupted him. "I promise you that if there's something I really need you for, I will make it clear. But if I tell you something like this, that if you're there, great, but not to worry about it if you can't make it, then I need you to believe me. I won't play games about stuff like that. I mean, I don't anyway, but especially not with you. You can trust me with that."

He sighed. "I don't deserve you."

She grinned. "Maybe I'm exactly what you deserve after some of the shit you've dealt with in your life. Also, your cheeks are really, really smooth."

"It's Magic."

"Magic?"

He laughed. "I get ingrown hairs if I use a razor, so I use Magic shaving powder." He reached behind him, opening the door without turning away from her. "I better get out of here or I'll start trying to convince you to change your mind."

"It wouldn't be hard to do. But this is smarter. Probably."

"I'll try and be here for dinner."

"If not, we'll figure something else out. Soon."

"My new favorite word," he said, then closed the door.

She leaned her forehead against it and listened to his footsteps retreating down the hall.

CHAPTER NINE

Rose woke to a new conundrum as an entrepreneur. To take a sick day or not. What had started as sniffles last night, that she'd blamed on the cold air, had bloomed to a full-fledged cold. Then she remembered that it was Saturday. At least there was that.

She staggered out of bed to check her medicine cabinet, and remembered that she'd pretty much thrown everything out when packing for her move or shoved it off on her friends. Ugh.

Pushing her glasses up her nose, she didn't even consider putting her contacts in. No way. She pulled on jeans, boots and a sweatshirt, yanked a knit cap down over her messy hair and trudged out. Vaguely noting that it was a pretty day, the snow sparkling on the mountains in a way that would normally have her itching to snap a picture with her phone, she made her way to Main Street and debated.

She needed to turn right, but if she stayed on this side of the street, she'd come to Starbucks. If she crossed the street, she'd reach the pharmacy. A round of coughs reminded her of the urgency of her mission, so she crossed the street and headed to Lavender and Mint. She passed by BBQ and Taphouse and made a mental note to try it out when she was feeling better, because it smelled delicious.

She passed the grocery store and opened the door to the pharmacy, sneezing into her elbow as the bells chimed.

Erin was helping someone at the pharmacy counter, so she checked the aisle signs until she saw cold and flu, then stood staring at the options. There were a lot. She didn't get sick often, so she didn't have a favorite brand or type, and just couldn't bring her brain around enough to decide what would work best.

An arm reached past her, picked a box up off the shelf, and stuck it in front of her face.

She looked up and dredged up a smile for Ben while accepting the box he offered.

"Thanks," she said, then promptly fell into a coughing fit.

Ben reached past her again and grabbed a bag of cough drops, which she also accepted. She saw a box of Kleenex, snagged that as well, and checked out.

She went to the grocery store next and got tea and honey, and had a long chat with Mrs. Rubinski as they walked home together. The other woman was wearing forest green slacks and a sage green sweater. Rose had forgotten all about her old teacher's penchant for wearing green. Where she'd found it eye-roll worthy as a teenager, she found it strangely comforting now. She took the medicine, then texted Ethan, letting him know that she had a cold, was medicated, and would be going back to bed, so there would be no lasagna that night.

When the doorbell rang, she had just changed into sweats. She narrowed her eyes at the door, then trudged to it. The peephole revealed her dad, carrying a sack.

"I heard you were sick," he said, brushing past her and heading straight for the kitchen. "I picked up chicken noodle soup from Sit A Spell. I'll just put it in the fridge for you."

"Thanks, Dad." She blew her nose.

"Want some company, or are you going to try and go back to bed?" he asked.

She had been thinking about going back to bed, but wasn't really tired. Unless the medicine kicked in and made her tired.

"Company would be nice for a while. Who's watching the store? I thought you were on for Saturdays."

"Your mother asked to switch with me for Sunday. She and her girlfriends are going into the city for a sale at some store, and Sunday worked better for the other ladies. I'll go in when I leave here, though, since Alex needed the day off."

She decided not to question, or comment on, the fact that this meant her parents would be working at the store at the same time. Clearly this was surprising only to her.

They moved to the couch and he tucked her blanket around her.

"It's almost spring," he said. "When you're feeling better, how about we go for a hike out on the other side of the river?"

She hadn't done that since she was in high school. "That sounds awesome, maybe Mom can cover for you on a Saturday or Sunday, to make up for today. Otherwise, I'll figure out what week I can do a swap and work a Saturday so we can go out on one of your days off."

"We'll work it out," he said, smiling.

Apparently she was more tired than she'd realized, or the medicine had kicked in, because she woke up some time later. The lights were off and she was stretched out on the couch, a glass of water and the box of Kleenex in easy reach on the coffee table. He was a good dad. She shot him a quick text to apologize for falling asleep on him.

She debated going back to sleep, but her stomach rumbled, so she shuffled to the kitchen and poured half the soup into a pot, managing to make only a small mess in the process. She was trying to decide how high to set the heat, which seemed super important to her sluggish brain, when the phone rang.

ETHAN WALKED out of Mrs. Rubinski's feeling optimistic that the new remote control would curtail the calls he got from apartment 114. Not that he minded, really, but it frustrated her that she couldn't get the television to do what she wanted, and he wanted to ease that frustration.

He bit into his cookie and checked his watch. It was almost lunchtime, and hopefully Rose had gotten some rest since she'd texted him that morning. He walked to Sit A Spell. In his opinion, the diner had the best chicken soup in town.

When he placed the order, the waitress asked him if he was getting it for Rose, then let him know her father had already taken her some.

"I'm going to grab you some of the garlic bread. Take that, she'll be happy for a little crunch and garlic's good for a cold."

He agreed to the suggestion and headed back to the building.

Fairly confident that Rose was someone who would put her phone on silent or Do Not Disturb when appropriate, he chanced calling her as he let himself in. She answered with a cough.

"Sorry," she croaked.

"Don't be sorry. I wish you were feeling better. Did you get some sleep?"

"A couple of hours."

"I heard you got chicken noodle soup from the diner. Would you like some fresh garlic bread to go with it?"

She sighed. "That would be nice, thank you. I was just heating up the soup. I'm sorry about canceling dinner."

He started up the stairs. "You'll just have to owe me one, I guess," he teased.

"Hey, you weren't even sure if you were going to make it or not," she protested.

"Then why are you apologizing?"

"Oh, whatever."

He chuckled. "You're too easy to tease when you're sick."

He put the bag down in front of her door and turned back to the stairs. "I'm leaving the bag at the door. I'd come in, but I can't risk taking any germs to my sister. I'm sorry."

"Oh no!" she moaned into the phone. "I didn't even think of that last night, when I had the sniffles. I should have."

He heard her door open, just before the stair door closed behind him. "Don't be silly. I didn't think you were sick, either. I just have to be a little more careful than normal. Please don't feel bad."

She sighed, and he heard the bag rustling. "Hang on, I'm putting you on speaker so I can put the phone down. Do you mind? Or did you need to go?"

Talking on the phone wasn't normally something he enjoyed, but she sounded bored and he felt bad that he couldn't go in and sit with her, so he dropped onto his couch. "Sure, I can talk a while. Did you have a nice visit with your dad?"

"For a minute, and then I must have fallen asleep. Which is a good thing, I guess. Now I feel like my head is full of slime." He heard the clinking of a bowl and spoon, and the rustle of a paper bag, probably the one with his bread in it.

"Yuck. Maybe time to try some more medicine?"

"I did, I think the new dose is starting to kick in now. Speaking of that, I went to the pharmacy and saw Erin yesterday."

"She had a rough time when she came back, but she seems like she's doing okay with it now. Her ex is kind of a twat, but people mostly ignore him."

"I want to hear more about Josh Harmon. The only visual I have is of a skinny little kid ice skating."

"Oh, yeah, he did love to skate, didn't he? Played a lot of hockey. I forgot about that. He's a good guy, it sucked to see him go through that, too. Everyone thought he and Patty were good, and then all of a sudden she was moving out, Bob was moving out, and the kids were just totally confused. They're so young, they won't even remember having been a whole family."

"Erin said people were being a bit hard on Patty, but now they're being more careful."

"Yeah, on the one hand they liked to blame Bob, since he was new to town, but on the other hand, I think the woman always gets more of the blame. Stupid. They were both assholes."

She chuckled, but it turned into a coughing spree.

"Anyway, Josh is a good guy, seems like a good father. He went to college in Denver, came back right away to be a teacher. I hear he's pretty well liked."

"Good. So he'd be a good match for Erin."

"Uh…"

"Why not?"

"You don't think that would be weird?"

She sighed. "Fine, who else would be a good match? She deserves some love in her life."

"Why does this seem like a trick question?"

He heard her spoon rattling in the bowl. "I don't know. I don't usually play matchmaker. I guess she just had a certain tone in her voice when she mentioned Josh, so it got me thinking. And maybe I had romance on my mind yesterday when I was talking to her, a little more than I usually do."

He should be concerned that she'd used the romance word. He *was* concerned. Sort of. But not in the panic-inducing way he should be. But he needed to be careful. The last thing he wanted to do was hurt her. So, while he wanted to tease her, he stopped himself.

"There are several guys around town who Erin might find interesting to date, and Josh is certainly one of them, but I'm thinking you should leave that up to her."

"Ha, that's what you think. I'm feeling the need for a girls' night out." She coughed again. "Well, not exactly right now, but soon-ish. Speaking of that. Um, do you think Alyssa would be interested in a girls' night?"

His breath left him in a whoosh. He should have seen that coming, but somehow it had blindsided him. "Well—" He cleared his throat. "She probably would, but it would have to be at her house. And couldn't be too long. Or too many people. But yeah, I think she'd like that. Her friends do still go see her, but it's usually a lets-go-cheer-up-Alyssa kind of thing. I think she'd like it if you told her you needed some help fixing Erin up with someone."

"Okay," she said softly. "I'll work on that when I'm sure I'm cootie-free."

"Okay. I'm actually going to need to go in a bit. I'm taking Jackson, Alyssa's husband, out for an early dinner while her best friend visits. He hardly does anything besides work and be with Alyssa, so Pam tells him she needs her Alyssa time, and I do my part to drag him out for a game of pool and then some BBQ."

"God, Ethan, I can't even imagine how hard this is." She sniffled, and he couldn't tell if it was the cold or tears.

"It pretty much sucks. She's fighting. He's fighting. We're all fighting for her."

"Yeah." It came out so softly he almost didn't hear her, but he felt her.

"Do you think you'll get some more rest?" he asked.

"Yeah, that's probably a good idea. I'm so thankful you brought the bread, it made the soup meal perfect. They say garlic is good for a cold."

"I'm glad. You take care of yourself."

"Okay, Ethan. You take care of you, too. I think you have a tendency to take care of everyone else."

"I'll try."

When he hung up, he dropped his arm to the couch and stared at the ceiling a while. She was right. He did have a tendency to take care of the people in his life. And he was pretty maxed out on that right now. So, what kind of sense did it make to invite someone new in? Someone who was considering leaving in just a few months?

CHAPTER TEN

Two weeks later, as Ethan watched Alyssa's shining, smiling face, he tried to remind himself of his need for caution. He'd been banished from the house when Rose, Erin and Anna arrived. He'd been worried that it would be too much, had warned Rose up to the last minute that if Alyssa wasn't having a good day, they'd need to cancel. She'd been perfectly fine with that, just like she'd been fine with him not coming around to see her for a week while she'd been sick.

He'd left them to it, with a promise from both Alyssa and Rose, separately, that they would text him if they needed him.

Now, their laughter greeted him as he quietly let himself inside. Jackson was at work, and Ethan had promised that he'd make sure Alyssa had a quiet night after the girls left. They'd brought all kinds of food with them, so he was sure there'd be some good leftovers.

The ladies were clearly wrapping things up, keeping to the timeline they'd promised him, which he appreciated. Alyssa didn't look tired at all, but it would catch up to her quickly.

He wished he could ask Rose to stay, but that wouldn't be cool. Other than a few texts and one quick phone call to arrange today's gathering, he hadn't had any time with her since their phone call. He wanted to see her. Wanted to spend some time with her.

Hugs and kisses were handed out as they filed past him to the door. Rose's hug was extra hard, and he found himself returning it in kind. "Can I call you later?" he asked.

"Of course." Her gaze searched his, then she was out the door. He stared after her for a moment, before Alyssa called his name.

He found her at the dining room table, leftovers wrapped up, no sign of dirty dishes.

"Hey, Lys. Did you have a good time?"

She smiled, held out a hand to him. He helped her rise and walked her to the couch. She'd lost so much weight. The dread that lived inside of him, the constant knowledge at the back of his mind that he pushed away, moment after moment, threatened to burst free. On days like today, when she looked relatively good, he forced himself to believe, despite her telling him the odds weren't good. But it was harder and harder.

"I did. It was nice to get to know Rose again. I thought she was so cool when I was a kid, going off to Los Angeles by herself."

"I'm glad you had a good time."

"My friends have been awesome through this, but it was fun to talk to some new people. Thanks for helping arrange it."

For some reason, he just couldn't pull out a smile for her. He loved her so much, had been taking care of her for so long, and there just wasn't anything he could do to make her better.

The look of understanding she gave him only made him feel worse. "It will be okay," she said softly.

He shook his head.

"It will. Life will go on. You'll have good times and bad times. You'll remember me. I want you to be happy. I need to know you'll be happy."

He shook his head again, completely unable to open his mouth. Unable to breathe past the lump in his throat. She'd never spoken so plainly about her own death before. He wasn't ready. She needed to fight.

She took his hand, kissed his knuckles. "You've always been there for me. I'll need you to keep doing that, when I'm gone. Keep being there. Keep living and loving and making me proud, like you always have."

He choked in a breath, but she didn't stop.

"I hate that I stole part of your life. You didn't go to college, didn't get out of here, find a wife, live a real life. You put your life on hold for me, more than once. I need you to promise me that you won't keep doing that."

"Lyss—"

"I want Jackson to find happiness again. I want you to tell him that, when the time is right. My only regrets are that you put off finding a family because of me, and that I didn't give Jackson children. But there's still time. I want you to love someone as much as I love him, as much as he loves me. I really, really want that for you."

"Honey, I didn't put off finding a family because of you," he managed to say.

"Maybe not consciously, but I think I was part of it. Me and Mom. You couldn't handle the idea of another person relying on you, counting on you to take care of everything. But it will be different when you find the right woman. A partnership. Promise me you'll try."

She was getting worked up now, leaning towards him, gripping his hand.

It took everything he had to choke the words out. "Will you keep fighting?"

"Oh, Ethan. Yes, of course I will."

"Okay. All right. I promise."

Settling back into the couch with a sigh, she closed her eyes and smiled. "Good. Thank you."

He turned the television on to whatever channel she'd left it at, some kind of cooking program, and waited as she fell asleep.

It was only nine-thirty when Jackson came home. Alyssa roused enough to hug Ethan goodbye, and he headed out. He was home within minutes, and nothing caught his eye as needing to be done as he went into the building. No messages on his phone, no requests for his time. He was tempted to go. Somewhere. Maybe just drive for a while.

Instead, he picked up the phone and hoped Rose would answer.

"Hey, Ethan. Thanks again for helping us set that up today. It was really great to spend some time with Alyssa."

"You stole my line. I'm sorry it's late, I just wanted to call and say thanks again for getting the girls together. Alyssa loved it."

"Then it was great for all of us. Hey, um, are you busy?"

He felt his muscles start to relax and took in a deep breath. "Nope."

"I have this thing. It's kind of a joke, so it's totally okay to laugh."

Intrigued, he sat up. "Okay."

"After we left Alyssa's, I went over to my mom's house. I'd never gone through my old stuff after I left for college, and she wanted me to see what we could get rid of. So, anyway, if you have, like, five minutes, could you come over? But I need ten minutes to get ready first."

"Sure. I have no plans."

"Great. But, remember, it's totally okay to laugh when you get here."

"Okaaaay," he drawled. "I'll be there in ten minutes."

He brushed his teeth, put on a fresh sweater, and made sure there were two condoms in his wallet. Just in case. Then he ate a cookie, so he wouldn't smell—or taste—like toothpaste.

When eight minutes had passed, he jogged up the stairs and knocked on the door to apartment 212.

The door opened a crack, but he couldn't see anything.

"One more reminder. Laughing is okay in this situation."

"If you say so." He was beginning to doubt the truth of the much-repeated statement.

The door slowly swung open. The light in the living room was off, but the hall and kitchen lights were on, casting the room in a dim glow.

But it was enough to see Rose, standing two feet in front of him, wearing a pale blue strapless dress, her hair up, baring her neck and shoulders. The dress nipped in at her waist and then flowed out with some sort of netting that also had sparkles on it.

Her prom dress. It had to be. He couldn't decide if he should laugh or cry. It was a fifty-fifty chance, which way he could go, and he was pretty sure he was just staring at her, wide-eyed, as his body tried to decide.

Then she stuck her tongue out at him.

The laughter burst from him, and he wrapped his arms around her, burying his face in her hair. He wasn't one-hundred percent sure that a sob didn't escape with the laughter, but hoped she wouldn't notice. She was giggling in his arms, and he managed to quiet down so he could hear the pretty sound. Which is when he realized...

"Is that the Backstreet Boys?" he asked.

"It is."

"And this is your prom dress?"

"It is."

"Wow."

He pulled back, hands on her shoulders, and looked at her. She was so beautiful. "I would have brought you a corsage if you'd given me a better hint."

"Totally unnecessary."

The music changed, and he cocked his head, trying to place the song.

"Kelly Clarkson," she told him.

"'A Moment Like This,'" he remembered. And took her in his arms, led her in a dance.

"Be careful of your hand on my back, I had to cut the zipper and safety pin an extra panel in. I didn't have as much boobage then as I do now."

She was laughing, but he wasn't finding the situation amusing anymore. He didn't know if she'd done this for him, for her, or just as a lark, but he couldn't tear his gaze from hers, couldn't stop from pulling her in closer, turning her to the slow beat of the music.

Her smile faded away and her eyelashes dipped as she watched his mouth.

He obliged her unspoken request, leaning down just enough to brush her lips lightly, all he would have been able to do on the dance floor at their school, many years ago. Then, with a wicked grin, he followed the music as it switched to a fast-beat song, pushing her into a spin, moving her around the floor to the sound of her breathless laughter. She wasn't a natural dancer, but she followed his lead as he followed the music, an eclectic mix of songs from their high school years that hadn't been lined up quite the way a DJ would have.

When another slow song came on, she sighed, leaning into him as he pulled her close. They swayed, his hands going around her back, hers resting on his shoulders. Slowly, he inched one hand down the curve of her ass, until he cupped the cheek.

She tipped her mouth up to his ear. "We'll get in trouble," she whispered.

"Nobody can see."

"Promise?"

"Promise."

She kissed below his ear, then nipped at his jaw. He squeezed the handful he held, pulling her in closer so she couldn't miss the hard length of his arousal.

"Naughty, naughty."

"It's your fault, entirely."

He wasn't sure if the music was still playing. The blood was pounding in his ears and the only thing he could hear was her whispered words. "Kiss me, please."

She didn't have to beg. He found her lips, pressed them open with his, and claimed her softly. Gently. Until her nails dug into his shoulders, sharp enough to feel through his sweater. Then he took. She moaned, her hand sneaking down to his waist, sliding up his bare skin.

He speared his fingers through her hair, pulled her back until he could see her eyes, drowsy with need. "Tell me how far you want to go."

"We're not in high school, Ethan. Start working your way to my bedroom or we're going to end up on the floor. Soon."

He laughed, bent, and scooped her up into his arms.

She squealed and clung to his shoulders. He might have worried about tearing her dress, but since she'd already taken scissors to it, he decided he was safe.

ROSE COULDN'T BELIEVE Ethan was carrying her to the bedroom. *Ethan Woodford.* High school quarterback, one of the most popular guys in school. Would-be prom date. Taking her to bed. He carefully angled through the bedroom door, succeeding in not knocking her into anything, then tossed her on the bed. She bit back a shriek as she bounced on the mattress.

She propped herself up on her elbows and watched as he toed off his shoes at the same time he gripped the bottom of his sweater and pulled it over his head.

Oh yeah. She sat up, sitting cross-legged with the fluffy skirt spread around her, and rested her elbows on her knees, her chin on her hands, enjoying the show.

Ethan paused as he started to unbutton his pants, and stared at her. She waggled her eyebrows at him. He put his hands on his hips and scowled.

"You're wearing a lot of clothes."

"Nope, just one dress. Well, and underwear."

"Okay, you're wearing a lot of fabric."

"What, you don't want to give me a show?"

"You left the music in the other room."

She leaned over and turned on her alarm clock. It was set to a classic rock station. She didn't recognize the song right off, and all ability to think drained out of her head when his knees suddenly dipped and he began to move to the music. Her mouth may have fallen open. He shot her a sexy teasing look, and she was thankful she was sitting down. And hoped she wasn't drooling.

He slid the pants down, taking his boxers with them, and she pulled her bottom lip between her teeth as she heard her breathing pick up. Turning, he looked at her over his shoulder like a pinup girl, wiggled his butt. She hadn't known you could be thoroughly turned on and totally amused at the same time.

"Oh, baby!" she called out.

He kicked his pants free, held his arms out wide, and spun back around to face her.

She put her hands over her eyes and gasped. "Oh, my, I just don't see how we're going to fit."

"Oh, we'll figure it out, I'm sure."

He grabbed her wrists, pulled her off the bed and onto her feet. "Are you going to give me a show?"

"I actually need your help to undo the safety pins on the back."

"What were you going to do if I didn't try to seduce you?"

"Is that what you're doing?" She grinned at him. "I hadn't actually planned to get naked, as hard as that is to imagine right now. I can technically do it myself, but it would involve some unglamorous contortions."

He let go of her wrists and she turned around. She felt the dress give on each side as he unclasped the pins, but didn't move when his large hands settled on her waist. Slowly, the dress dropped away, and she was wearing only her panties and his hands. She felt sexy and seduced.

His hands moved up her back, curved over her shoulders and down her arms. Clasping her hands, he raised them up, then turned her, moving to the beat of the music she'd forgotten. He brought her forward, so her nipples were just barely touching him, teased by the motion of their bodies as he guided them in small circles.

"The last thing I thought I'd be doing tonight was this," he said softly. Then he grinned. "Well, that's not exactly true. I was thinking about you. And I might have had thoughts about sex and you. But I never imagined you in my arms like this, all soft and sexy and sweet. Wearing that dress. *Not* wearing that dress."

"I'm just glad you didn't think I was being a dork." She'd really been worried about that. Or of bringing up bad memories that he wasn't ready to set aside.

"If you were being a dork, it's definitely the kind of dork I like."

She narrowed her eyes at him. "Hmph."

He laughed and pulled her in tightly, dropping his hands to her ass. Then he lowered his head and kissed her, and she stopped wondering if she should be annoyed. She stopped thinking at all.

His fingers squeezed, their tongues tangled, their bodies heated. Before she knew it, she was moaning his name, pulling him towards the bed. He resisted, and she nearly protested when he let her go and turned away, but he only went as far as his pants, pulling them to him and grabbing his wallet.

Oh, yeah, good thinking.

She climbed onto the bed and he tossed a condom on the mattress, then followed her up, stretching out beside her, propped up on one elbow. He watched her face as one hand drifted lazily over her thigh, up her side, circled her breast. She bit her lip as his fingers played with her nipple, then gasped his name when he leaned in and sucked it into his mouth.

He played with her breasts until she couldn't stand it anymore and pushed him onto his back. He didn't take much convincing. She slid over him, her palms learning the shape of his chest, her thighs bracketing his.

"You are so sexy," she breathed.

"Now that is definitely my line."

"Don't argue with me."

"Yes, ma'am."

She smiled and slid her hands down, wrapped around his length, exploring the shape, squeezing when his legs tensed like he was going to move. He cursed when she bent down to lick. She tasted and explored until he growled at her. "Come here."

Moving up his body, she met him for the kiss, unsurprised when he turned them, so she was once again on her back, his full length stretched out over her. He kissed her until she was dizzy with it, while his hand teased her into mindless need.

Finally he pushed back, quickly put a condom on, and slid into her in one even thrust.

Her legs came around him, pulling him in as tightly as she could.

"You feel so good," he said.

"I—" She broke off with a gasp when he moved just so. "Share that sentiment."

He began to move faster, working to a rhythm she couldn't hear, but she followed his lead and met him stroke for stroke until she couldn't hang on any longer. She flew, holding him tightly to her, anchoring herself in him until she landed. Blinking her eyes open, she found him watching her.

"Damn," he whispered. "That was beautiful. You're beautiful."

She slid her hands down to his butt. "Show me yours."

He grinned at her and resumed his thrusts, peppering her face with kisses until he shoved his face into her hair and groaned his release. He rolled partway off her, but she didn't let him move far. They curled into each other, sweaty and warm and very, very satisfied.

Her mind drifted in a warm haze. Sixteen years ago she'd wondered if she might lose her virginity to Ethan on prom night. It wasn't expected, but it wasn't completely unusual at her school, either. The chances had been slim for her, though. She wasn't ready. And they'd never even been on a date. Her friends who were considering it had been with their guys for at least a year, working their way through the bases.

So she hadn't really thought it likely, but for the first time in her eighteen years it had been conceivable. She'd thought of him, just for a second, the night in college when she did have sex for the first time. Then she'd pushed him out of her mind, mostly, until she'd started making plans to come back to Colorado.

Now, here she was, lying in bed with him. And not the boy she'd known. No, she was all about the man he'd become. His fingers had started gliding up and down her arm, side and hip. Strong fingers, a little bit rough from all the work he did. She shivered.

"Cold?" he asked.

"Nope."

He yawned. "That was a much better end to the evening than I'd expected."

"How was Alyssa?" she asked. She should have asked earlier, but she'd been too worried that he'd take the dress thing the wrong way.

His fingers clenched against her side for a minute, then resumed their path. He didn't say anything though, just shook his head.

Crap. She wished there was something she could do. For Ethan and Alyssa.

There was a tension in him now that wasn't there a minute ago. He clearly didn't want to talk about it. And if that was the only thing she could give him right now, it would have to be enough.

"I talked to Naomi and Janelle today. I had to show them video evidence of the dress."

He relaxed again.

"Were they impressed by the fashion sense of eighteen-year-old Rose?"

"Of course, though they said I could have spent more time on my hair."

"I can't say I noticed that."

"You're such a guy."

"Thank God."

She laughed. "Yes, thank God."

"Anything new with them?"

"Tony the Asshole has been relatively well behaved lately. Nell thinks he's probably getting good sex, so hopefully that will last a while."

"Hopefully."

"Nay's having to evict her first tenant, and she kind of hates it but is enjoying a little vindictiveness because this guy's really been a jerk."

He shuddered. "I hate that. Second worst part of managing tenants."

"What's the worst?"

"Trying to figure out who's lying about needing help and who really does."

"Like, help with their rent?"

"Yes. I don't mind letting someone go a couple of months if they need it, but I really, really hate trying to figure out who's scamming me and who's really in need. If I could just believe them all, it would be fine. But I also hate being taken advantage of."

"Oh. Yeah. I can see how that would suck."

She yawned and he rolled her over and lay mostly on top of her. "I'll head out. Let you get some sleep." He dropped a kiss on her lips.

"Okay. This was nice."

"Definitely my kind of nice. Let's do it again."

"Okay."

He laughed, gave her one more kiss, then rolled off the bed. He gave her a cheeky little butt wiggle as he headed to the bathroom.

CHAPTER ELEVEN

Ethan checked the supplies in his truck and turned to Rose, who'd walked with him to the coffee shop and back, so they could start their day off right. She sipped from her cardboard cup, the steam rising in the cold morning air when she pulled the cup away. His was already empty. It had been nearly a week since she'd invited him down to see her prom dress, and their schedules hadn't lined up well, so this morning they'd settled for coffee.

"Cable, come-along, wedges, chainsaw, gloves, helmet, goggles. I think I'm set. You get back inside and warm."

"I feel like I know what all the words you said are, and yet, I'm clueless. You said you're helping the town mechanic take down a tree?"

"Jake, yeah. He has one that's dying and he's worried it might fall on the house if it comes down in a storm. It's leaning towards that direction. So we need to take it down and we'll use this stuff to make sure it doesn't fall on the house when that happens. He's giving me a free oil change in exchange for helping out and bringing this stuff. Which reminds me, do you need an oil change?"

"Wow. That's so mountain-man manly."

He laughed. "I'm glad you think so. I think."

She smiled. "And no, Janelle took care of my car when I was in Los Angeles, and she gave me one just before my trip."

"I thought she worked for Tony the Asshole as some kind of executive?"

"She does, but she decided to learn how to take care of cars to save herself some money, and ended up liking it so much she does her friends' cars, and her friends friends' cars, as a sideline."

"That's handy." He leaned in for a kiss and she lifted up on her toes to receive it. "I'll see you later." He watched until she was at the door and turned to give him a wave before he got in the truck and headed to Jake's house. He turned left on Main Street, past the Tavern, Masonic Temple and McDonald's. There were two cars in line at the drive-through as he passed. A quick right onto Grizzly street and he could see that the garage was closed, probably with a sign giving Jake's number and saying he'd be back in the afternoon.

He turned onto Owl Lane and into Jake's driveway. The older man with his bushy beard and coveralls came out as Ethan closed the truck door, and immediately moved to the back of the truck to start hauling out the supplies. Two dogs were on his heels, acting like they'd be helping too. Jake shooed them off as he and Ethan loaded up and headed to the back of the house.

Ethan had come out last week to look at the tree and plan their strategy, so they were able to get to work pretty quickly. They'd chosen the direction they wanted the tree to fall, and picked two healthy trees to use the cable and winch with to force the issue. Jake put the dogs into the house and Ethan fired up the chainsaw.

It didn't take long to bring the tree down, and they worked quickly together to get it into pieces that they stacked up for Jake to deal with later. Jake would let the wood cure a while before he and his son Jasper chopped it up into logs that would fit in the living room stove for winter heat.

"I hear you're seeing that Rose Chapman, come back from Los Angeles now," Jake said as they heaved a piece onto the pile.

Ethan stood up, looked around himself at the woods. "It's funny, it doesn't *look* like I'm in a beauty shop."

"You're a funny man."

"If you say so."

"I'm just saying, she's a nice girl. Done well for herself out in the city, there, from what I've heard."

Ethan felt his shoulders tense. He'd never been warned away from a woman before, and he wasn't sure how he should respond.

"I haven't talked to her myself, so I could be wrong, but it seems like she'd be good for you, Ethan. A woman who knows how to take care of herself, but can also be a partner. A man has a partner at his side, it makes going through the days a whole lot easier."

"All right, Jake. I appreciate the advice. I'll keep it in mind. Now, what color are we going to die my eyebrows?"

Jake threw him an amused look but shut up and moved back to the woodpile.

Ethan thought about the conversation on his way back home. It was nearly one and he wondered if Rose had already eaten lunch. He used the handsfree to send her a text asking, and was receiving a reply as he jogged up the steps at Salmon Springs.

No, just about to take my break, if you're here, come on up!

He was knocking on her door three minutes later with a six pack of Cokes he'd stopped to grab from his fridge. She didn't seem to notice the drinks, as she hauled him in for a kiss the minute she opened up.

She groaned, and pulled away too soon.

"Lunch. I have frozen burritos or I can make ham and cheddar cheese sandwiches."

He offered up the six pack. "Sandwiches are good, I'll help.

"What's on your schedule for the rest of the day?" she asked as they got started with that.

"I need to do some work at the apartment." He tried to judge how much there was to do. "I don't think I'll be done in time for dinner, but maybe dessert? How's your day looking?"

"I'm really close to finishing a project, so I'll probably work until it's done, instead of just knocking off at five. If I haven't heard from you, I'll go into town for dinner. I'll need to walk around a bit after sitting all day, for sure." She put the top pieces of bread on their sandwiches and grabbed a bag of chips. "And then we'll see about dessert."

They moved to the table and both attacked their sandwiches like they hadn't eaten for days.

"I'm excited about being done with this project," she told him between bites. "It's been interesting, and I think the client will be very pleased with the results, and will hopefully pass that along to some people they work closely with."

"Nice."

"The guy there, who's my main contact, he's a veteran, and that got me to thinking. We absolutely do not need to talk about it if you don't want to, but I thought I remembered hearing, as a kid, that your dad was military? That he died overseas?"

He finished the chip he was eating and nodded. "Yeah, he was. I know everyone whose parent died fighting says they were a hero, and maybe they are, but he had awards and medals. He was the real deal and he was a good father and husband. He set Mom up so she didn't have to work after he died. There should have been enough money to take care of us, take care of her."

"Should have been?"

"His brother, and my mom's family, they all suddenly were entitled to a little bit here and a little bit there after he died. Guilting my mom into spending our money to pay off this medical debt, bring that mortgage up to date. That kind of thing. She figured out pretty quickly they were just going to nickel and dime us into poverty, so she packed us up and moved us here. She and my dad had seen a postcard of Wildlife Ridge one time and thought maybe they'd like to raise their family there when he got out."

"Wow, that sucks that instead of supporting her they were going to slowly bleed her dry. It's good she was able to walk away from them. How old were you when you moved? I don't remember you ever not being here."

"I was four. Alyssa wasn't even six months old when Dad died."

"Oh, Ethan. That must have been so hard for your mom."

"Yeah. Her mom was on her side, encouraging her. Grandma Patrice. They would talk on the phone every day until she died when I was six. We went out for the funeral, and that was the last time Mom left Wildlife Ridge, or talked to the rest of her family, as far as I know."

"That's awful. You never hear from them?"

"Once in a while someone reaches out, but honestly, I don't even respond. I just have no interest in finding out what kind of people they are these days." He felt like he should apologize for that.

"Of course not. Maybe someday you'll feel like seeing if you have cousins who aren't assholes. And maybe you won't." She shrugged.

He breathed easier. "Mom didn't really start drinking until I was in elementary school, and even then it wasn't bad until later. Alyssa and I talked, when I started high school. By then I was handling all the bills and finances. The house was paid off and we thought there was enough money to take care of mom, but we weren't sure there would be enough to do that and pay for college for both of us. We decided we'd do scholarships and loans for us, if it meant we would never be faced with having to pay for her needs out of our own pockets."

He took a long drink of his Coke. "Which ended up not mattering after all." He pulled out his phone. He'd set up a video camera and recorded the felling of the tree, and the process up to it, but he'd taken a couple of shots with his phone, too. "Here, you can see this manly mountain man in action."

"Jake?" she asked, eyes opened wide to feign innocence.

"Yes, Jake. I have a crush on him and am trying to entice him away from his wife." She giggled as he showed her the pictures, his body slowly relaxing when she leaned into him to get a closer look, laying her head on his shoulder.

"Wow, that beard is something else."

"We discussed dying it pink," he lied.

Her laughter washed away his old pains.

CHAPTER TWELVE

Rose hit send on her email and sat back. She'd completed the project she'd mentioned to Ethan, and it felt amazing. She checked the clock on her monitor. Five-thirty. Earlier than she'd expected. But, she realized as she stood, she had definitely been correct to think she'd need to go for a walk once she was finished. Talk about being stiff. She needed to get better at moving around every hour or so while working. She took off her glasses and rubbed her eyes.

Working from home was going really, really well. She'd actually let herself say no to a project, because it would have meant a lot of late nights to complete it as well as keep up with the projects she'd already committed to. It had been super hard to say no, but she kept reminding herself that her business wasn't brand new, she already had a name and reputation built, and though she was trying to grow it, there was a limit to how fast she could do so without compromising her work-life balance.

Still, it had been scary to let the potential client know that she'd be happy to take their job in three weeks if they still needed her, but she couldn't take it on at this time.

She checked her phone, in case she'd missed any messages from Ethan. No message, so she would go for that walk to stretch out her muscles and get some dinner. Her neighbor Claudia was heading out as well, so rather than take the stairs, Rose joined her in the elevator and they had a nice chat about a documentary they'd both heard was good and wanted to watch. They separated at the front steps so Claudia could get her car and Rose headed towards Main Street.

She decided she needed to walk more before eating, so Rose turned left, away from the restaurant. Ethan had mentioned they'd put in a little dog park out by Bighorn Automotive, so she headed that way. The sun was getting low, setting the mountains off beautifully, and the air was crisp and clean. She really was glad she'd come here. Los Angeles certainly had its own charms, but this was a beautiful place to live.

It was hard to believe a month had already passed. She was just getting into her routine, and wasn't at all ready to start researching other places to live.

She wandered past the vet's office, and paused at the little bookstore-coffee shop. Two nights ago she'd spent a hilarious evening with Cal, Jin, Mayor Shirley, Ben from her yoga class and Trisha from the bakery doing a painting class. They'd each brought a bottle of wine to share and had a blast pretending they knew what they were doing. Actually, that wasn't fair, the instructor had done an excellent job of getting them to produce something they felt good about, and she was debating between hanging the little painting or giving it to her mom. Moms loved that kind of thing, right?

She waited for a bicyclist—was that Sandra, the bartender from Wolfhound Tavern?—and jogged across Main Street, then hooked right to walk up Grizzly Street. At the corner of Grizzly and Boars Tusk Road, the garage was on one side and the park on the other side. A chain-link fence surrounded the large park, as well as splitting it off into two areas. Signs indicated that one section was for small dogs, the other for large dogs. Trees at the far end of the spaces made it look somewhat park-like, but the main section was mostly dirt, with a bit of snow. Dogs were running about, some barking, some chasing balls. It looked like a lot of fun. She watched a puppy in the large-dog area as it tried to chase some of the older dogs and fell head over heels, rolling back to its feet without pause.

Oh, man, they were so cute. She'd always wanted a dog, but it was definitely not in line with her plan of being able to travel. Maybe her long-term plan, she decided now.

A couple with a German Shepherd on a leash were exiting the park, and she took a second look. If she wasn't mistaken, that was Harry Khalid, the boy who'd taken her on her first date. Which would make the woman with him his wife Pam, Alyssa's best friend.

Harry saw her, and raised a hand. "Rose!

She waited for them to reach her, and to be introduced to Pam, before crouching down to pet the gorgeous dog.

"This is Pete," Harry told her. "He's not shy about licking faces, so be careful."

Since she was currently dodging such a licking, while giving the dog a good ear scratch, she just rolled her eyes. "He's beautiful, how long have you had him?"

"Two years now, give or take. We wanted to wait until our youngest was in school, and then we rescued Pete. He was three, then, because I was not going to deal with a puppy," Pam told her.

She gave one last rub of Pete's head and stood. "I can't believe your kids are that old now. You have a boy and a girl, right?"

Pictures were produced on phones and she spent a few minutes oohing and aahing over the adorable kids who were now seven and nine.

"Alyssa had a great time with you all the other day. Thanks for making that happen."

"We *did* have a great time, I wish you could have made it. I hear you're an optometrist in the city? How's that commute?"

"It's not terrible. Every so often I think about trying to open an office here, but the numbers haven't seemed quite right. So, for now, commuting is the only option if we want to keep living here. Which we do."

"I didn't expect to dislike my time here, of course, but I've been a little surprised how much I've enjoyed it, after getting used to Los Angeles."

"You're not planning on staying, though?" Harry asked.

"I was planning on researching cities to consider while I was here, but I haven't been doing much of that. Maybe I'm getting sucked in," she laughed. "Who knows? Or maybe I'll travel around and come back. That's the good thing about this job, I can do it from anywhere and not have a commute."

"I'd be jealous, but I actually love my job," Pam said.

"I'm so happy for you. It's rare to hear people say that."

"I know. Harry isn't in love with his admin job, but he can't decide what he wants to try and do, either."

Watching the way he was with Pete, she said, "I'm sure you've thought of this, but what about something with animals? You seem to have a way with this one." The big dog was leaning against Harry's side, attentive but completely calm.

"Yes, I've considered it, but it comes back to the issue of what this town is big enough to sustain. Unlike my wife, I don't love driving in snow, and I do love living here, so that limits my options. The good thing is, I don't hate my job, so I'm fine with keeping on with it while I think about things."

"That's good," she agreed. "I was heading down to Quail's Nest for dinner, just taking the long way. "Do you guys want to join me? I can wait while you take Pete home."

"Thanks, but we'll take a rain check," Pam said. "Harry's mom wanted to make the kids dinner, but she'll be about at her limit soon. She can only handle them on her own in short doses."

Rose laughed. "All right, some other time."

They all looked up as a car, painted to look like a shark, drove by. It had a fin on top, and large pointy teeth at the grill. She blinked and looked to the couple who were laughing at her expression.

"That's David," Pam explained. "the real estate agent who works next to the hardware store?" She continued when Rose nodded. "He loves to paint, and he had an older car that needed some paint. One thing led to another, and he started painting the car to look like animals. He changes it up every month."

"He has a regular car, too, for when he meets with out of town clients," Harry added.

"Wow, okay then. Whatever makes someone happy, right? And it looks amazing." She hugged them goodbye and retraced her steps, past Dragonfly Road, where her apartment was, and past the library and post office. She was walking past Starbucks when she heard her name being called, and saw Erin hailing her from the pharmacy across the street.

Waiting for a break in traffic, she jogged across the street. "Hey, I was heading to Quail's Nest for dinner, you free?"

"Sure, Livvy's at her dad's. I was just waiting for my assistant to come back from break and then I'm off. Can you give me five minutes?"

They were on their way shortly, crossing the street again and going into the restaurant. It was crowded, apparently the warm day had brought out the tourists. Despite that, they were seated within a few minutes and Rose took a look around.

"I've never been here, but I heard the food is good."

"It's great. It was okay for a lot of years, but then they got a new chef a few years back, and it's really stepped up several notches. The prices went up a little, but not terribly. And if the waitstaff know you, they actually give you a locals' discount." She said the last part quietly, since the booth next to them was clearly filled with tourists.

"Ha, that's pretty cool." Rose pointed her chin at a family of three nearby. "Okay, I swear I remember babysitting for the Bakshis when I was in eighth grade, and their son was a toddler. Who's the girl? She delivered my pizza my first night here."

Erin grinned. "Good memory, sort of. You did babysit Davey when he was a toddler, but when he was in seventh grade, he let his family and the community know that he was Dara from now on.

She's a junior now, and yes, working as a delivery driver for City Pizza."

Rose blinked at her for a second, and then grinned. "My observational powers are clearly not great, although in my defense it would be hard to recognize anyone who was three the last time you saw them."

"True. The town has done really well to not make a big deal out of it. There are only a couple of old coot assholes who insist on calling her by her old name."

"And none of the bathroom issues that seemed to be plaguing our nation not too long ago?"

Erin rolled her eyes. "No, I've not heard of anyone at the school giving her grief over going to the girl's bathroom. She has a good clique of friends, though I haven't heard of her dating anyone yet."

"I'm glad to hear the town is reacting well," Rose said as she scanned the menu. "Anything I just have to try?"

They debated items on the menu, questioned their waiter, who Erin introduced her to, and finally ordered.

"Who else can you catch me up on?" Rose sipped on her Diet Coke and scanned the restaurant.

"Hmm," Erin murmured, looking around as she considered. "My husband cheating on me with the neighbor's wife was honestly the biggest news around for a long time. He swears she's the only one, but I'm not convinced he and Tilly Green over there never had a thing. I used to tease him because she was always flirty with him. She's a single mother, and she'd do things like ask him to reach something for her on the top shelf at the grocery store, or help her carry something to her car. Gave him the delicate-female-to-macho-male routine. Which is all fine, in theory, but if Bob and I were in the aisle, and Donna Calender were there, she would ask Bob instead of Donna, who's actually taller. That kind of thing, which made me wonder if I was paranoid."

Rose glanced over, as nonchalantly as possible, to check out the woman who looked to be about her age. She was dressed in a business suit, her dark blonde hair up in an elegant French twist, and was chatting with her dinner companion, an older woman who could be her grandmother.

"Skank, clearly," Rose said, dryly.

Erin rolled her eyes and laughed.

"Where did she come from?" Rose leaned forward on the table. "There must be something juicy."

"She transferred in with the bank, about three years ago. Nothing too exciting, I'm afraid. You're in Salmon Springs, right? She's in one of the Beaver's Dam buildings. I can never keep them straight. I don't know who thought it would be a good idea to name one building Beaver's Dam Court and the other Beaver's Dam Manor." She shook her head. "Anyway, I heard she was looking at one of the rental houses."

"How's the market out here, do you know?"

"It's not cheap, but better than in the city. My cousin in Denver pays about the same as I do for my two bedroom house, for her two-bedroom apartment. And not one of those fancy apartments with concierge service or anything like that."

"Interesting. My friend is a landlord, so I pay a little bit of attention, though I've never wanted to deal with that kind of investment myself."

"I used to think it would be great if we had duplexes or triplexes here, buy one of those and rent out the other units. Then I remember that I hate having to deal with anything to do with the house, and that I should stick with what I know. Which is the pharmaceutical industry, not real estate."

Rose leaned back in her seat as the waiter brought their dishes. "I bet you could learn it if you wanted to, but I don't think it's something people should get into unless they have a real desire for that kind of work."

"Probably. And I keep pretty busy with my work, and Livvy. I was able to buy the pharmacy last year, when Doctor Eller retired. It's been different than I imagined, going from being an employee to running the whole store, but I like it. I just want to make sure all of my eggs aren't in the same basket."

"Sounds like a good case for a healthy 401K?" Rose asked.

"Exactly. It was easier when I worked for a big company, and they handled all the hard work with that. But, then again, now I get to make all the important choices, instead of relying on management to know what they're doing, and that doesn't suck."

Rose waved her fork at Erin and nodded. "Nice. And so is this pasta. It's delicious, actually. Want a bite?"

"I won't say no, since I was tempted to get that for myself. But you should try the risotto, it's fantastic."

They ate in appreciative silence for a few minutes, before Erin's phone dinged at her.

"Sorry, I know it's rude, but I always check when Livvy's not with me."

"No problem, check." Rose took another bite and watched as Erin pulled her lip between her teeth and nibbled on it. The other woman did a quick few clicks on her phone, then put it down on the bench beside her.

Rose didn't say anything, just raised her eyebrows and gave a knowing look. No way that text was from or about the kid.

"My, um, neighbor. Just texting me to let me know he pulled my garbage can up, so I wouldn't worry when I got home that it had been absconded with."

"Absconded. Your word, or your neighbor's?" she teased.

Erin blushed. "His."

"Uh huh. Your neighbor. I'm guessing this is the teacher neighbor. The handsome teacher neighbor, Josh? Unless your other neighbor is a police officer."

"Oh, all right, yes it's Josh, and yes, he's been more friendly lately. We had dinner!" Erin's eyes got wide and she glanced around to make sure no one was checking out why her voice had gotten so loud.

"You're fine, no one's listening except me. So tell me everything. I'll spring for dessert, you dish up the entertainment."

"Ha, ha. It was totally innocent. He came home and found Bob next door with Livvy. Bob had gotten confused and thought he was bringing her to the house instead of the pharmacy, and he had to get to a meeting, so Josh offered to bring her over."

"I'm surprised Josh would even talk to Bob."

"Me, too, to be honest. I actually asked him about it. He said he is disgusted by both Bob and Patty, but he knows that it upsets the kids to see tension, so he just had to decide to not hate them. It's pretty much how I've dealt with it too, so I understand. I mean, it would be easier to be hateful to Patty, since I don't have to be nice to her for Livvy's sake, like I do Bob, but that would just be stupid. And he agrees. We're not going to be buddies with the exes like some people are, but we're both doing the best we can to co-parent, and we appreciate that both are decent parents, not like some of the nightmares you hear about."

"You guys talked about all of that? While Livvy was there?"

"Well, Livvy and his kids went into the living room to watch a movie after dinner."

"So, him bringing Livvy to the pharmacy ended with dinner at your house, with his kids."

"Well, he went to pick up his kids and when we got home, they were playing outside and Livvy wanted to join in. They were having a lot of fun, and working up an appetite, of course."

"Of course."

"I offered to make dinner while he watched the kids, if they all wanted to join us."

"Bravo."

"I just...when I think about it, I think it's a really bad idea. To date, I mean. Or consider a relationship. Why open myself up to that kind of heartache again? Livvy and I do just fine on our own, and between her and the pharmacy I have plenty to keep me busy."

"Your marriage wasn't all bad. You had to have had some good times. It doesn't make you want a partner again? A real one, not someone pretending to be one?"

"Maybe, if I had the confidence that I could tell the difference this time."

Rose frowned, wishing she could think of some way to reassure her friend, but she didn't exactly have much experience in successful relationships to draw on.

"The thing is," Erin continued. "When I'm with him, I stop thinking about it being a bad idea. I just think of how nice it is to have adult conversation at the dinner table, along with the fun patter of the kids. To have a second set of eyes on the kids while they're playing, in case I want to run into the house to use the bathroom."

She paused and scraped up the last of her food while Rose polished off her bread.

"And he's a nice guy. He makes me laugh." She shook her head. "I guess what I'm saying is that when I'm with him, I'm not really thinking about relationships or the future or how much gossip there would be if we got together. I'm just…enjoying myself."

"I think that's awesome. And I don't think you need to change anything, or make any decisions. Why overthink things? Just enjoy yourself, and if the time comes to take things to a different level, it will happen, or you'll decide it shouldn't."

"That sounds easy. Easy to say. But I've, uh, maybe been having inappropriate thoughts about him."

Rose watched the blush climb up her friend's face and cleared her throat, trying not to giggle. "Like, at night?" she asked, just to be sure.

Erin buried her face in her hands, her shoulders shaking in laughter. "Yes, of course at night! I remember, after the divorce, thinking it was funny that I didn't even miss that part of my relationship with Bob, even though we'd had a decent one. Honestly it just hasn't been on my radar the last two years."

"Until now."

"Until now." Erin dropped her hands and took a long drink of water.

"Well, I guess that means part of you *is* ready to take things to another level."

"Right. Hence the overthinking."

Rose nodded. "All right, I get that. But I would bet money he's thinking the same thing."

"Maybe. Probably. Or not. Maybe."

Rose laughed and accepted the menu from their waitress who chose that moment to come by and ask if they wanted dessert.

"Oh, yes, Erin has definitely earned dessert for tonight."

CHAPTER THIRTEEN

Ethan hung up the phone after talking to Jackson and immediately called Rose.

"Hey," she answered.

He'd missed her voice. He'd missed *her*. Which was kind of crazy, they'd had a couple of quick phone calls but he hadn't seen her since lunch the other day. And, considering neither of them was supposed to be interested in dating, that should be fine. Funny how it didn't seem to be all that fine. At least to him.

"Hey. How do you feel about *The Karate Kid*?"

"The movie?"

"Yep. They're showing it at the MacAllisters' tonight. Alyssa's had a good day, so she and Jackson are planning on going."

"Oh, wow, are they still doing movie night in the basement? That's awesome."

"Still doing it, although the MacAllisters don't live there anymore. The Silvermans do, but the MacAllisters left everything behind and the Silvermans kept up the same tradition. Mostly in the winter, when it's too much of a pain to drive to Bell View to see a movie, so this is probably the last one they'll do for a while. They might throw in a summer movie for fun."

"I'm totally in. I have a yummy recipe for caramel popcorn, and it only takes a few minutes. I'll bring a huge mess of that."

The way it worked was that those who could, popped a couple of dollars in a coffee can on the way in. It was a donation, not required, but most people contributed every movie or two. That way the furniture and blankets were replaced before they were old and ratty, and basic supplies like paper plates and napkins were always on hand. Everyone who could also brought extra food or drink. If they ended up with way too much perishable food, the Silvermans donated it to one of the local congregations.

"Perfect, I'll grab a six pack of beer and soda and pick you up in twenty minutes?"

"I'll be ready."

She met him at the stair door on her floor, and they walked the easy ten minutes to the Silvermans' house. It had been a sunny day, but he suspected there would be snow falling by the time they walked home. That was okay, they both had boots and layers and would be fine for the short walk.

They chatted about what they'd both been busy with all week until they ran into Cal and Jin, also walking to the movie house.

"I haven't seen this movie in years," Cal mentioned.

"I'll bet you five dollars you've never seen this movie at all," Jin challenged.

Cal opened his mouth to argue, then frowned. "Wait, do you mean they're showing the remake? You're right, I've never seen it. I assumed you meant the old one."

"I did too," Rose muttered.

Ethan laughed. "You should have asked. I bet you'll have fun with this one, too. Besides, isn't it more fun to see a movie you haven't already seen?"

They made their way inside. He found that Alyssa and Jackson were already there, and surrounded by friends and neighbors they hadn't seen in a while, so he didn't bother trying to get seats near them. The available options were the floor with pillows, a couple of beanbag chairs, or a love seat. Rose grabbed his hand and beelined for the beanbag chairs, dropping his hand as she fell into one with a giggle.

"Man. I haven't sat in a beanbag chair since…well, maybe since being here. Maybe even this particular chair, the way it feels now." She scooted around, trying to get comfortable. "No, that's better," she said, once she had everything positioned correctly.

She was only settled a minute before jumping up to hug one of their high school classmates.

He watched her, smiling animatedly, filling the woman in on her return to Wildlife Ridge. They gave a quick hug when the lights flashed, indicating that the movie was going to start soon. He looked around as she plopped back into her seat. The basement was full to capacity tonight, with about twenty people. It was a huge space, which is why it had always worked out for movie night, and why the community had been pleased when the Silvermans bought the house and said they would keep the tradition going.

He settled back in to watch the movie, casually reaching over to take Rose's hand in his when the lights went down. She squeezed his fingers and angled her body more his way, finding a comfortable position to keep her hand in his while watching the large screen.

When the movie was over, they hung around a while, discussing the quality of the remake over the original, as well as the current gossip, with the others who lingered. Alyssa and Jackson had left as soon as the movie finished, but Jackson's look had reassured him that Alyssa was fine, she hadn't overdone it.

Ethan suddenly realized that chatting with his neighbors wasn't really what he was in the mood for. He wanted to be alone with Rose.

He caught her eye and gave a subtle head tilt towards the door. She smiled and began putting on her jacket, gloves and scarf while saying her goodbyes. As expected, it was snowing when they stepped outside, and she wrapped her hands around his arm and snuggled in close.

He liked it. A lot. He liked *her*.

They strolled easily back to the building, not rushing. When they got to her floor, he tugged her to a stop before she went through the door that exited the stairwell.

"Come up to the roof with me. We can watch the snow."

She blinked at him for a second, then smiled. "Okay."

He didn't move, captivated by that smile. It did things to him. Made his heart feel…mushy.

"Well?" she asked and gave him a little shove.

He huffed out a laugh, grabbed her hand and pulled her up the stairs. He'd never brought a woman up to his roof. Or a tenant. It was his own private space in the building that he'd never considered sharing before. But he'd made some preparations after calling Rose about the movie.

So when they stepped out onto the roof, fairy lights twinkled around the porch swing he'd set up a couple of years before. It was the kind with an overhang, so, if the wind was cooperating, and it seemed to be, they could sit without too much snow falling on their faces.

He led her to the swing and, while she sat, opened a weather-proof storage locker that he kept next to the swing, doing double-duty as a side table. He pulled a furry throw blanket out and draped it over her. Then he produced two wine glasses and handed them both to her. From beside the chest, he picked up a bottle of white wine. Opening the screw-top lid with an exaggerated flourish, he filled both glasses.

"Wow, aren't you fancy?" she teased, snuggling into him as he put the bottle onto the chest and took his seat next to her.

"Once in a while."

They leaned back and watched the view. The rooftop was the tallest vantage point in town. Depending on his mood, and the wind, he sometimes moved the swing around. There were moun-tains no matter which direction you looked, but right now they had a pretty view of the town nestled into the trees. Most of the housing developments were here, on the north side of Main Street, but when they looked beyond the row of lights that came from the businesses lining Main, he could see the lights of the sawmill in the far corner of town, backed up against the highway. Next was a small housing development, and last the scattering of cabins and more isolated houses. All a pretty twinkle, this time of night. He wouldn't call the sawmill pretty during the day. He did appreciate that it was close to the onramp for the highway, so it was rare for the chip trucks to clog up Main Street too much. For Wildlife Ridge, a traffic jam was waiting for one car to turn out of the grocery store at the same time someone else was trying to turn into BBQ and Taphouse next door.

They sipped their wine and watched the lights in town slowly disappear as it grew late. He didn't feel the need to fill the silence with words. He supposed he should have brought a radio up, or set a playlist on his phone, but he kind of preferred the silence broken only by the occasional sounds of life, a dog barking, a door slamming.

A car started up a couple of blocks away, the sound easily traveling in the cold, dark night. "That will be Donna Calender, heading to the city. She's seeing a guy who works nights, so she takes a nap after dinner and then heads out his way."

She sighed. "I should be horrified that you know that, probably half the town knows that, but I find it sweet, instead. Something must be wrong with me."

"She told me all about it the other day."

Rose laughed. "Of course she did. Did you guys ever date?"

He scrunched his nose. "No, we never had that kind of vibe for each other. She calls me if she has car trouble or to let me know that she's making my favorite cookies for the church bake sale, and to come get the extras before she takes them over."

"That's nice." She lifted her glass to her lips and he just watched her while she watched the snow falling over Wildlife Ridge. Well, until she gave him the side-eye and he faced forward again, his arm wrapped around her shoulders.

"Did I tell you my mom and I went shopping at Costco?" she asked.

"I think you mentioned it. I never shop there, doesn't seem to make much sense for a single person. Did you guys split things?"

"Yes, that was the plan. Only, it turns out, she's been splitting with someone else. They went in together on the membership last year, for this very purpose."

She said it in a meaningful tone, so he studied her face, but he couldn't think what that expression could mean. "Who is it?"

"My dad!"

"Huh."

"Yeah. I mean, all this time I thought they could barely speak to each other, and they're working and shopping at Costco together."

"Wow. Well, they're working at different times, though, right? And do they actually go to the store together?"

"No, my mom does the shopping and splits everything up and he pays the membership fee. They do work different hours, but when Alex was off recently, they were at the store at the same time."

"Interesting. How do you feel about this…cooperation thing they seem to have going on?"

"I'm glad about it, obviously, it's just weird. I mean, when I first came back to town, my mom and I had a conversation about the divorce. She told me things hadn't been quite the way I'd thought they were when they split. So that was good, because I'd thought my dad had been an ass. Turns out that wasn't exactly the case."

"That's good. I've always liked your dad. I don't dislike your mom, I mostly just try to avoid her."

He was worried she'd take that the wrong way, but she just laughed. "I get that. When I first came back she also mentioned that she'd offered you time to work at the store and you'd turned her down. She was shocked that you would turn away good work. Of course, then she offered me the same, and was equally appalled that I turned it down, too. *The kids these days*," she sighed, before drinking more wine.

He laughed. "I don't know why she has the impression I need work. I guess because I like to help people with odd jobs when they can't do them on their own, she thinks I need money? As opposed to thinking that I like to offer my skills to those who don't have them, or don't want to pay someone from the city to come in and do it?"

"I think that's pretty much it. Personally, I think it's awesome that you're so helpful, as long as you're not letting people take advantage of you."

"I love being part of the community. Not just living here, but actually participating like that. It makes me happy."

She smiled up at him and kissed his lips.

He eyed their glasses. Maybe a couple of more minutes and he'd suggest going back inside, even if they hadn't finished.

"You're right," he continued, "it can be easy to let people run roughshod over your free time if you're not careful. I bet you get requests from people to do computer stuff for them all the time."

"Yep."

"Since I do the handyman thing, I have to balance being helpful against being taken advantage of. But so far, I'm managing it, and enjoying it. It sort of helps that I do have that reputation for not making commitments. Like we talked about before. Maybe, unconsciously, I've even fostered the idea, so that I'm able to keep my balance."

He met her gaze and forgot if he was going to say something else. He forgot everything except the taste of her lips. He needed to check, make sure he remembered correctly. Or see if she tasted like caramel popcorn. Or pinot grigio.

Her eyes got a little bit wider as he leaned in, but then her lashes drifted down. He touched his tongue to her lip, just barely, but that wasn't nearly enough. He pressed his lips to hers, gratified when she opened for him immediately.

She gave a tiny little moan and he speared his fingers through her hair, her knit cap falling to the side. Unlike him, she still had her gloves on and they rested against his jacket. He needed to get her inside, where they could be wearing a lot fewer layers. Wanted to feel her hands on him. But he didn't want to stop kissing her, not just yet.

His phone rang. At first, he didn't really register the sound. But when it rang again, he groaned. Shit, shit, shit.

He pulled free and watched Rose's face as he yanked the phone out of his pocket. Her eyes opened, looking dazed.

"Sorry, honey." He glanced down at the screen, worried it would be Alyssa or Jackson. But it wasn't it; it was Ian.

A call at this time of night, from Ian, could only mean one thing.

Shit. He stared at the screen, debating.

"It's okay, Ethan, go ahead and answer. It's after ten, it could be an emergency if someone's calling you now."

He sighed and pressed on the screen. "Hey, Ian."

It only took a minute to confirm that the call was exactly what he'd thought. "I'm not sure I can do that right now, Ian. Give me a minute, and I'll call you right back." He didn't wait for Ian's response, he just hung up.

"Every few months, Ian calls if Royce Rodgers has had a few too many, and it's busy enough that Ian can't drive him home. I could ask him to call Tom and Shirley, I bet one of them could take Royce home. Or Ben Ratcliff. It's only a ten-minute drive, it's just too far for him to walk it when he's in bad shape. He's out on Jackalope, on the other side of Town Hall."

"Don't be silly, they might already be in bed, and we're up." She glanced at the wine glass she'd set aside. "But I've finished my wine, so I probably shouldn't drive."

He turned to the glass he'd set on the chest. It was three-quarters empty, and he showed her. "I can drive, if you're sure you don't mind. And you can wait at your place."

She hopped up off the swing. "We'll go together. We needed to head inside soon anyway. Thank you for bringing me up here. It's beautiful, and I enjoyed seeing the view in the snow. Maybe I can come back sometime when it's clear and see the stars?"

"It's a date," he said, pulling her in for another kiss. He forced himself to keep it short, then gathered up the wine bottle and glasses while she folded the blanket and returned it to the chest. As they walked to his apartment to drop off the wine, he called Ian to let him know they were on the way. Rose handed him her keys so they could take her car instead of his truck, and they headed off.

CHAPTER FOURTEEN

Rose was slightly bummed at the interruption, because she'd just been thinking that they needed to move things inside and start losing some clothing, but she knew it wouldn't take long. And she was positive they could easily get things back on track, once they returned.

But part of her was getting a kick out of the small-town moment. In LA, if a bartender had been on the ball enough to know a patron was too drunk to drive home, they would have just made the person order a ride home or call a friend. But chances were good they wouldn't have even noticed, not until the person was falling down drunk, long after they were unsafe to drive.

She didn't love that Royce, who she vaguely recalled as being an attorney, seemed to have a drinking problem. But she did love that the community made sure he stayed safe.

The snow was barely falling by the time they got in the car. The drive to the Tavern only took two minutes, and Ian had Royce outside, by the door, waiting for them. Rose got out of the car and met him on the driver's side. They walked up together, and Rose could see that Royce was uncomfortable.

"I'm sorry, Rose, Ian shouldn't have dragged you out here like this."

"It's not a problem, Mr. Rodgers, we were out and just about to head home when Ian called. It's no big deal to run you home real quick. I hope you're feeling okay."

Royce ran his hand over his head, then down his face. "Aw, now, you can call me Royce. You're not kids anymore. And I'll be fine, I just need to get some sleep now. I should have headed home a while ago, but I got caught up watching the game, I guess."

She held out her arm to him. "All right, Royce, let's get on the road then. It was nice to see you, Ian." She tossed the last part over her shoulder as she and Royce made their way to the car. He didn't really seem all that drunk to her, which made her more pleased that Ian had been paying attention to how much the other man had been consuming.

When she tried to lead Royce around the front of the car to the passenger seat, he protested and insisted she sit there, then climbed into the back behind the driver's seat. By the time she made it to her door, Ethan had it open for her. He put his hands on her shoulders and kissed her, right in front of everybody. Well, everybody being probably nobody, as Royce couldn't see and Ian had gone back inside. But it was possible other people were out and about on the streets.

He let her go, and she whispered, "That was nice."

"There's more of that to come. Shortly. I didn't want you to forget in the meantime."

"Very thoughtful of you."

She slid into the seat, waiting until he'd shut the door to put her seat belt on. Turning, she made sure Royce had put his on, too. The man's eyes were closed, and he looked sad.

She flashed a look of concern at Ethan, but he just shook his head, put his own seat belt on, and backed out of the parking space. She tried to think of something to say, but she was worried she'd bring up the wrong topic, since she clearly didn't know what was going on. Probably should have asked more questions on the ride over.

Royce didn't seem to mind the silence. They drove up Main Street, turning onto Elk, which circled around the town hall. Since it was a one-way loop, they had to follow it all the way around to the other side, to make the turn onto Jackalope. They didn't pass a single person along the way, and the snow had completely stopped falling by the time Ethan pulled up to the first house on the left.

A subtle look and hand gesture was all Ethan needed to convince her to stay in, since she was pretty sure it was more about taking care of Royce than just saving her from having to get out of the car.

"It was good to see you, Rose. I'm sorry about dragging you away from whatever you should be up to right now. I'm sure I'll see you later, and we can catch up some."

"That would be nice. You have a good night, Royce, and get some sleep now."

"I'll do that."

He closed the door gently behind him, worried, she knew, about how far sound carried in the still night air. She watched Ethan put his hand on Royce's shoulder when they got to the door, leaning in to speak to him. Royce nodded, opened the unlocked door, and went inside.

Ethan looked tired as he headed back to her, and she wondered if he'd want to change his plans now that they'd finished their mission. But then he looked up, met her gaze, and suddenly he didn't look tired at all. He looked like he wanted to get her on a bed, stat, but had no intentions of wasting time sleeping.

She licked her lips, losing sight of his face as he reached the car and ducked back inside. He put his seat belt on and stared straight forward.

"I'm not going to kiss you right now. Otherwise, we'll be necking in a car like teenagers in half a minute, and I don't think you want that."

She opened her mouth to agree, then paused. "Actually, I never necked in a car as a teenager. Almost, once, but we got spooked by another car driving past, and we gave up. It might be fun."

He looked over at her, a pained expression on his face. They were on the outer edge of town, in an area that would have some good turnout locations. He'd probably gone necking back here when they were younger. She'd have to ask him about that sometime, but for now, she didn't leave him in suspense.

"Some other time, though. Take me to your place, Ethan, I want to see your bed."

The relief on his face was short lived, as it morphed into determination. He drove carefully and steadily, and they were parking at Salmon Springs only minutes later. He made it around to her side of the car by the time she was carefully putting her feet on the ground, making sure it wasn't icy. She took his offered hand, closed her door and grinned at him.

"What are the chances that we'll make it to your door without someone stopping us and asking you for help or a favor of some sort?"

His face fell.

"No," she assured him quickly, putting her hands on his face, making sure he was looking at her to see how serious she was. "I was teasing. Stopping what we were doing to help Royce was a good thing. The fact that people know they can turn to you for help is also a good thing. I am *not* upset in the slightest. I'm happy I was able to come along with you. I promise."

His worried eyes softened as she spoke, then heated as she finished her little speech and continued to stare at him.

"Take me upstairs. And if someone interrupts us, we'll see if we're on the same page about what kind of priority their request is at. If Mr. Brown needs a ride to the hospital, we'll take him. If Mrs. Rubinski needs her TV remote to be fixed, we'll swing by, because that takes two minutes. If her sink has a little leak, you'll tell her you'll be there bright and early in the morning. How's that sound?"

"I bought Mrs. Rubinski a new remote. She hasn't had any problems yet. It's maybe a little bit too early to call for sure, but I think that situation has been solved."

He smiled as he said it, and she pushed up on her toes to give him a quick kiss. "Excellent."

"But if it hadn't, I would have put her off until morning."

Rose laughed. They made it to Ethan's apartment without running into anyone, so no need to test priorities. Rose was glad. She was positive they would have been on the same page about anything, but she was just as happy not to have any interruptions as she was to prove to Ethan that she understood what it meant for him to be an active member of the community. She was proud of the place he held, and wondered if there was some way to convince him that people didn't see him the way he thought they used to.

As soon as they cleared his door, he locked it and the heat in his gaze ratcheted up by a factor of one hundred. His look alone took her breath away, so she made no move as he grabbed the end of her scarf and slid it through his hands, then tossed it on the couch. He had her coat off before she blinked. She finally kicked into gear herself and worked her boots off while he dealt with his own coat and boots.

Then they were in a mad tangle of hands and arms, trying to take off sweaters while kissing, unbuttoning jeans while trying to be as close to each other as possible. When Rose almost fell as they pushed and pulled at each other, Ethan cursed and lifted her up against the wall, her bare back meeting the chill of the surface, her legs wrapping around his hips.

He supported her with his hands under her butt, pinned her with his lips against hers, his tongue doing that delicious tangled dance that made her ache down below. She cupped his head, scratching through his short hair with the tips of her fingers, wringing a moan from him that made her smile against his mouth.

One hand left her butt, but she felt secure. Until he used a finger of his free hand on her clit. She gasped into his mouth, the little motions of his finger making her breathe faster and faster, swirls of delight erupting in her stomach. Squeezing her thighs around him, she pulled her mouth free, pressed her head back against the wall, elated when he slipped a finger into her core, sliding in easily through her wetness, his thumb continuing to work her clit.

Magic, she thought. He had magic fingers, magic tongue, magic hands holding her, bringing her up, hard and fast, in a way that usually only she could manage for herself. She wanted him inside her, not just his finger. She tried to tell him that but her words strangled on a gasp as he somehow managed to bend enough to pull her nipple into his mouth, laving it with his tongue, then giving her a gentle bite.

She moaned as she came, the release soft and sweet, but leaving her empty and aching at the same time. He seemed to understand, because he pulled her from the wall and staggered down the hall. Or maybe it was her heart beating so hard that made them seem to stagger, since he appeared to be carrying her with ease. When he came to a halt, she lifted her eyelids, not having realized she'd closed them, and eased her legs down.

He held her until she was steady, then reached behind her to pull a condom from a bedside drawer.

"How many more of those do you think you have in you?" he asked, a teasing light in his eyes that made her smile.

"I have no idea. Let's find out." But then, just to be contrary and answer that tease with her own, she bolted to the side.

She didn't make it far, giving a light shriek as his arm banded around her waist. He lifted her off her feet and tossed her to the bed. She rolled with the bounce and came up off the other side. "Gonna have to catch me first, though."

He glanced over his shoulder at the door, making it clear there was no way she would make it there. That was okay, she had no intention of getting away. He eased toward the end of the bed and she hopped back on top of it, giving a little bounce.

"It's like that, is it?" he asked, mock seriousness in his voice.

"You have to work to get what you want, right?"

"I don't know, seems you got what you wanted pretty easily out in the living room."

She moved her gaze down to his cock. "Nope, still haven't gotten what I want, but I'm not too worried about that."

His grin turned fierce and he leaned down, both hands on the bed, fisting into the comforter. She had one bare second of understanding before he pulled the blanket out from under her, toppling her to her back.

She was laughing as she came down, expecting to bounce, but instead he was on top of her before the momentum could carry her up, his heavy body an exquisite weight that made her breathless again.

Wrapping her arms and legs around him so he couldn't get away if he had a mind to, she arched into him as much as she was able.

"Ethan," she moaned.

"Mm, say it again."

"Ethan, I need you inside me."

"That's fortunate, because I need to be inside you. But first, I want to taste."

"Later."

"Now."

He moved down easily, despite her clinging limbs, and licked a circle around her nipple, first one, then the other. He teased and tasted, explored and nipped, until she couldn't think, could barely breathe.

"Ethan," she tried again, her head thrashing about on the pillow. "Please." She didn't know how long she'd been begging. Wanting. Needing.

"Soon, baby. Let me play a little more."

"My. Turn," she panted, though she had no strength in her limbs to do anything.

"Yes. Definitely your turn. All for you." He breathed the words along her skin, as he continued to stroke and taste.

"Noooo." That wasn't what she meant, was it? So hard to think, so hard to remember what she'd wanted. Her toes curled as his lips came to her center, and he spent more time tasting and exploring.

She bucked under him, a little frisson of heat shooting from her core to her belly.

He moved, and she tried to clutch him close but her legs felt like spaghetti, and since he moved up to kiss her, she couldn't really complain. His fingers eased into her, hooking just so to tap against that special spot inside of her.

The release took her fast and hard, a gasp that was lost in his kiss. Slowly, she lifted her eyelids, blinked to find him watching her, a satisfied little grin on his face. Maybe she should be annoyed, but there was really no way to pull that kind of effort out of herself, so she just watched his handsome face for a minute.

His arm moved, and he brought something up in front of her face. She blinked again. It was the condom.

"My turn," he said, his grin turning wicked.

She sighed, flopping her arms and legs to the sides in a starfish position. "Okay. Fine. Have at me."

He laughed, and then he did just that.

She found her second—or was it third?—wind and pushed him over, explored and tasted for herself. She ran her hair over his chest to tickle him, then lower. When he was panting hard, they went up on their knees, hers on a pillow to bring them closer in height, her forehead resting on his shoulder so she could watch as he stroked himself. He dropped back on his heels and helped her straddle her knees around him, drop down to cover him fully.

"Oh, Rose. So fucking good."

The reverent tone of his voice, the fullness inside her, his fingers digging into her ass, she held on to all of it as she held on to him. She met his gaze, and he was there, as if he'd just been waiting for her eyes, her soul, because that's what it felt like. Like her soul was open to him in a way she'd never known was possible. Her whole self was in her heart, in her eyes, as she looked deep into him, and felt herself give. Give all that she was in a way that should be terrifying, if she could just think.

But she couldn't think, could only give, only receive, only move in rhythm with Ethan as he began to slowly thrust, in and out, his gaze never leaving hers. Their breaths mingled and their hearts beat as their slick bodies danced. When, at last, it was too much, she had to drop her head back down and bite his shoulder to keep from coming, waiting for him, wanting him.

"Go," he panted.

"You," she insisted.

"I'm ready. Go."

She threw her head back and let it go, let the wave crest, taking her with it. She heard his shout, dimly, his arms banding around her, holding them steady as he released into the condom.

They dropped carefully to the side, rearranging the mess of arms and legs until they were comfortably entwined, their breaths slowly easing, hearts finding their regular rhythms, separate but together.

CHAPTER FIFTEEN

E than was determined not to let the day go by without seeing Rose. He still had a hard time believing how amazing their night had gone after the interruption of driving Royce home. And Rose hadn't minded. Sincerely. She'd been proud of him for being the person who was known for helping. He liked being that person, but he'd convinced himself that it came with the price of not being able to always keep a partner happy.

It was possible that he was an idiot. Or that he'd dated mostly idiots, back when he'd actually dated. Or that he just had a skewed vision of adult women, due to his mother.

Any of those were possible, he mused as he put the snow shovel away and checked his watch. Rose had stayed the night on Friday, and he'd made her breakfast Saturday morning, but she'd had to run to meet up with her father for a hike along the river, and he'd had to work on an apartment, so they hadn't seen each other all day.

But she'd knocked on his door at seven to see if he wanted to share the frozen pizza she was carrying. He had, though they hadn't done so until nearly ten. She'd given him a last kiss after they'd cleaned up dinner, told him she'd be running errands most of the day, and then yoga at four. She'd said that some of the class had made tentative plans to go to dinner afterward, but nothing concrete, and invited him to join her for the class, or just join them for dinner.

If he left now, he should be able to help Alyssa with the surprise dinner she was planning for Jackson, then meet up with Rose and either join the group, or take her off on her own if they had changed their minds.

Of course, things did not go according to plan.

When he arrived at Alyssa's, she was tired and cross. Which was unusual for her, so he guessed that she was in more pain than normal but refusing to admit it. It wasn't her usual MO, but it happened occasionally. Eventually he eased the truth out of her, and they called her doctor, adjusted her meds for the day, and he got her to lie down.

He texted Rose.

Was hoping to walk you to yoga and stay and watch you bend and contort, but Alyssa's having a bad day. Won't be able to make the may-or-may-not-be dinner, either. Sorry.

Don't apologize, that's crazy. Tell me the truth, would it be good if I came over there or bad?

He'd known, or mostly known, that she wouldn't be mad, but it hadn't occurred to him that she'd want to come by. Which showed how much he wasn't thinking straight, because of course she'd offer.

She's taking a nap now but I want to stick around in case she wakes up before Jackson gets home

Then how about I come over and keep you company? If she wakes up and wants space, I can leave. If she doesn't wake up, you're not alone.

He swallowed past a weird lump in his throat.

That would be nice. I'll be here several hours if you want to wait and come after yoga.

I'll be there in ten minutes. I'll put together something simple we can make for dinner and we can cook it up so it's ready for them, whether I stay or not. Nice and easy. See you soon!

He didn't bother to answer because he was positive she didn't expect one, and he really just wanted to hug her. Which he did when she knocked on the door nine minutes later.

She wrapped her arms around him, banging his butt with the grocery bags hanging from her wrists, and he didn't mind at all.

"What time will Jackson be home," she asked.

"Right about six."

"Okay, so we have some time. This will be an easy dinner, nothing fancy."

He'd texted Jackson to fill him in, before he'd texted Rose, but he hadn't told his brother-in-law about the surprise dinner Alyssa had been hoping to make. Hopefully tomorrow would work out for that. So he pushed the ingredients for that meal to the back so they wouldn't be super obvious to the other man.

He led her to the living room, falling into the couch, only now aware of how tired he was.

"I shouldn't be this tired. *Alyssa* is tired. Her body is fighting so damn hard."

"Don't compare, that's just silly. You're both allowed to be tired."

"I know. I just hate this so much. She's trying..." His throat closed up and he squeezed the hand he suddenly found thrust into his.

"It's bad," she said quietly.

He turned to face her, and the compassion on her face helped him say the words. "No one says it. Her doctors don't, Jackson, me. Alyssa tried to tell me, the other day. About a future without her." He shook his head, wrapped his arms around her when she climbed into his lap. "She's not going to make it. We all know it. I think her friends, the community, they probably still believe. They figure as long as they keep giving hope and prayers and frozen casseroles, she can keep fighting and beat it back, like last time. But they're wrong. She's so tired. She can't fight forever."

She didn't say anything, just held on to him as tightly as he held her, and listened.

"I'm watching her die...and it's tearing me up inside. I can't do anything to stop it."

"No, but what you *are* doing is so important."

He managed a tight nod. "I was always there to fix her problems, though. That was the one thing I never failed at. The one commitment I never passed over, no matter what."

He felt something on his neck, and it took him a minute to realize it was her tears. He blinked his own back. Now that he'd started talking, he needed to keep going. He hadn't been able to say these things to anyone, not even think them to himself.

"She was my little girl, you know? Sometimes I'd be annoyed when she wanted to tag along, but not mostly. Mostly I was glad she'd rather be with me than Mom, at least as we got older. I'm the one she came to when she was hurt or upset. I couldn't always fix it. I know that. But a lot of the time I could. If it was possible, I did. I liked being that person for her."

He pulled in a deep breath, focused his attention on her hand on his shoulder, slowly moving back and forth to soothe him.

"I was so happy for her, when she met Jackson. Once I decided he was good enough for her, I mean." He gave her a wry smile.

"Of course," she murmured.

"But there was that tiny part of me that was sad she wouldn't need her big brother anymore."

"Perfectly natural."

"When she got sick the first time, we all worked together. I mean, of course she had the hardest go of it, but I was so glad she had both of us."

"It's a lot, taking care of someone going through that. I can't even imagine."

"Yeah, it's a lot. But she never gave up, and I was so proud of her." No amount of blinking was going to keep the tears back this time. "But she's ready to give up now…and I can't blame her. I want to tell her it's okay to give up, but I can't seem to do that, either. I don't know if I'm failing her by thinking she's lost the fight, or if I'm failing her by pushing her to try harder, fight longer."

"Oh, Ethan."

Her body was shaking in his arms. Or maybe he was the one shaking with his tears.

"I don't want her to die, but I don't want her to hurt anymore."

"I know. It's okay. I know."

She held on to him, head resting against his shoulder, sniffling. He reached behind him for the tissue box resting on the console behind the couch and brought it forward. She took one, and so did he. His phone buzzed as he was wiping his nose, and he glanced at it in case it was Alyssa in her room, or Jackson checking in. It was a tenant, so he put the phone aside.

"Thanks for listening to that. It's hard to hear, I know."

"Harder to say."

He nodded. "Jackson will be home in a while. We should start dinner."

"You haven't talked about this with him."

"No. We both know that we both know, but we won't talk about it."

She sighed in his arms, and he knew she understood.

"Tell me what you need tonight," she said.

"I want to go sit on the roof and watch the stars for a while. That's it."

"You need to eat."

"I don't think Alyssa will be up. I'll be able to tell if Jackson wants company. If he does, will you stay and eat with us? If not, maybe we can grab something easy on the way home."

"That's doable."

They worked well together in the kitchen. She'd brought the makings for quick spaghetti, so he started a pot of water to boil while she chopped up some mushrooms to add to the jar sauce she'd brought. She put the mushrooms on while he chopped garlic. When he threw it in, she opened the package of ground beef, and dumped it on top. He stirred and stabbed at the beef until it started to cook and break up.

They heard Jackson drive up, so he dropped a kiss on her cheek and went out to meet his brother-in-law.

Rose used the selfie camera on her phone to make sure she didn't look like a raccoon while Ethan was checking in with Jackson, then gave her nose a thorough wipe.

She put the pasta into the water and shook the jar of sauce into the skillet, with the meat. She peeked through the cabinets until she found a colander and put it in the sink.

She couldn't say she was surprised by what Ethan had said, but she was definitely heartbroken. She hated that he and Jackson were in so much pain, but hated more that Alyssa was going through something so awful.

When Jackson came into the kitchen, after talking to Ethan and checking on Alyssa, he thanked her for making the dinner and asked her if she'd like to stay. She wrapped him up in a hug and told him of course she would. He gave her an extra-tight squeeze and she almost started crying again, but, knowing he didn't want that, she managed to pull it together.

The meal was the guys being mostly quiet, with Rose prattling on about her work and her old life in LA. She told them about being super proud to move into her first apartment without a roommate, before realizing that spending forty percent of her paycheck on rent was extremely stupid. She'd gotten a raise shortly after, and it would have been expensive to move, so she'd stuck it out and ended up living there for ten years. The rent had only gone up a little, but her promotions and raises had gone up a lot, which had allowed her to save money.

"You weren't tempted to move when you got raises?" Jackson asked.

"Sometimes, sure. But then I would look at my 401k balance, and run a calculation on where it would be in twenty years if I kept upping my percentage saved, versus if I stalled out or backtracked, and the different numbers were more than enough to convince me to keep going. It's not always about the numbers, but it brought me to here, where I can start making changes with my today, because my future is already assured. And that makes me feel great."

Jackson nodded and gestured to the house around them. "We

probably shouldn't have bought this house. The numbers weren't right, but we wanted to start a family, and we figured we'd both be getting raises, and it would all work out. We ended up getting Alyssa's inheritance and just paying it off after all, but technically we could have made smarter decisions."

She put her hand on his arm and repeated, "It's not always about the numbers."

He nodded and looked down at his plate.

She threw a panicked look at Ethan, but he just smiled, so she relaxed. Sort of.

She moved the conversation, which was eighty percent her anyway, on to the local gossip. They finished up shortly after that and made quick work of the cleanup. She gave Jackson a hug good-bye, but he was already looking towards the bedroom. She bundled up and walked out the door with Ethan.

"Want to get a hot coffee for the walk home?" he asked.

"That sounds nice."

They did just that, and made it back to the apartment building the same time as Anna returned from dinner. She gave Rose a quick hug and rubbed Ethan's arm.

"I'm sorry you missed yoga and dinner. We'll do it again, soon."

They said goodbye at her floor but kept going up, heading straight to the rooftop without saying a word. She took a seat on the swing, letting Ethan retrieve the blanket and tuck it around them before snuggling in close. The view was incredible. A perfect, clear night to see the stars. She rested her head against his shoulder and just watched for a long time.

"Do you know the constellations?" he asked finally.

"Hmm, Orion I see, over there." She pointed. "I think that's Cassiopeia, over there."

"If you follow Orion's arrow," he pointed, drawing a line to the right and down a bit, "there's Mars. And if you keep going past Cassiopeia, there's the Little Dipper."

She sat back and let him show her more stars and constellations, as the lights in the town started to go out, one by one. Eventually, she yawned one too many times, and Ethan put the blanket away and escorted her to her apartment.

"Do you want to stay the night?" she asked sleepily.

"I don't want to mess up your work morning."

"You won't, unless you initiate a sexual marathon while I'm sleeping."

"I promise to only initiate sexual marathons while you're awake."

"Then we'll be fine," she said, grabbing his arm and pulling him into the apartment.

She went into the bathroom to do her nighttime routine and came out to find him sitting on the end of the bed, the covers pulled down, wearing only his boxers. He watched as she went to her dresser and pulled out a fresh nightie, and turned to face him. She was pretty sure they weren't going to have sex tonight, which she was fine with. But that didn't mean she couldn't make him smile.

She slowly undressed, picked up the lotion on top of her dresser, and proceeded to apply it to every inch of her skin. He watched without saying a word, his eyes following the paths that her hands made. True, this was her usual routine, though she often followed it up with just a t-shirt, but usually she was much quicker and more economical with her movements.

But standing naked in front of him, wearing only the lotion she was applying, his warm regard made her feel as beautiful as if she had spent an hour dressing and making herself up.

She slid the nightie over her head, its hem falling to mid-thigh. The cinnamon-colored satin piece had been a gift from Janelle for her birthday, and she would have to remember to thank her friend later, as she was appreciating the affect it was having quite a lot.

Adding lacy panties ended her little show, and she walked slowly to stand between Ethan's legs.

"There's a toothbrush on the counter for you. Do you need anything else?"

"No, I'm good. Thanks for the show."

His hands came to her hips, resting against the satin, warming through to her skin.

He leaned in and pressed his face to her stomach, taking in a deep breath. She scratched lightly at his scalp, slow, easy circles that soothed her as much as she hoped it soothed him. After a minute, he eased back and stood, his hands holding on until she had stepped back enough that he could walk around her to the bathroom.

***

He did wake her up, not long before her alarm was set to go off. Long enough to make her wet and ready and hungry for him, begging him to slide into her. He did as she asked, her heels digging into his ass, her moans urging him on, until she came with a small burst that energized her.

Now that was a way to start the day.

CHAPTER SIXTEEN

Ethan found his days passing in a blur of work, yoga classes with Rose—seriously, how had he ended up being one of the bendy people?—pub nights with Rose and their friends, dinner dates with Rose, rooftop snuggles with Rose, bedtime romps with Rose, and hours spent with his sister. Sometimes with Rose, but often without.

Two months had flown by without his realizing it, before Alyssa asked him about Rose's lease.

He blinked at her. "It's for six months."

Alyssa sighed. "Right. And she's been here for three months."

He felt something weird in his chest at that. "She hasn't said anything about leaving."

"Has she said anything about staying?"

"She wouldn't just leave. Her work is going really well."

"I thought the point was that she can do that work from anywhere."

"It is, I just…"

Alyssa put her hand on his arm. "Ethan, I want you to promise me something."

She gave him a look that said he'd better be paying attention.

161

"Talk to her. See how she's feeling about it. But, if she needs to leave Wildlife Ridge—hell, even if she just *wants* to leave Wildlife Ridge—and you love her, promise me you'll go. Don't stay here just for me. I know you'll come back to visit when the time comes. It's not like you don't have enough money to fly in when you need to. So promise me you won't put your life on hold waiting for me to die."

He swallowed hard. "We're way ahead of ourselves here. It's way too early to be talking about love. And I have no idea if she'd want me to go with her."

She gave him a look to make sure he knew that wasn't the answer she was looking for. "Okay. If it gets to that…I promise—" He had to stop and clear his throat. "I promise that I won't put my life on hold waiting for you to die."

She watched his face, and then nodded, apparently satisfied with that. He was grateful she hadn't caught the fact that he hadn't said anything about leaving. No way in hell was he leaving before…well. No way was he leaving.

He went back to the apartment and picked up Rose and her car, because she wanted to do a big grocery shop. She had picked some tricky recipe for them to try together for dinner.

They moved down the aisles, following her shopping list, but when she almost passed the health and beauty aisle, he gave the cart a little tug and moved her to the condoms. As he grabbed a box, he glanced at the home pregnancy tests. He'd never paid much attention to them, never really given any thought to having kids, beyond buying condoms.

For the first time, he wondered what it would be like to be a father. To be a partner with Rose in raising their children. A little girl, like Alyssa had been. One who could grow up to get sick, like Alyssa had…

A stupid lump formed in his throat, and he grabbed the condoms and tossed them in the cart, giving Rose a tight little smile and nod, letting her know they could move on. She gave him an odd look, but returned to her list.

He followed along, the image of a little girl with Alyssa's curls and Rose's eyes stuck in his head. An image of him teaching her how to build a birdhouse, the first project he'd ever completed on his own. A little boy who had Rose's nose and Ethan's long fingers, sitting in his mother's lap, learning to code.

When Rose gave him another strange look, he realized he wasn't paying enough attention to what she was saying. He shook the images out of his head and tuned back into her. They finished their shopping and headed home, organizing the ingredients they would need for the meal.

They were just getting started with the prep when his phone buzzed. He groaned when he saw it was one of the tenants, but quickly answered. "Hello, Mr. Brown."

The conversation was short, but his stomach churned. He hung up the phone and turned to find Rose with one bottle of cider open next to her, and another, unopened, in hand.

"You have to head out?" she asked.

"I'm so sorry, Mr. Brown's toilet is leaking. It can probably wait until morning, but I should check, just in case. And if I'm there, and it just needs a seal to be replaced, it's better to go ahead and do it now. It shouldn't take more than half an hour. Unless it's a different issue altogether. It's possible—"

He broke off as Rose smiled and put a finger over his lips. "Ethan, there's no use guessing what it might be when you can just go downstairs and find out. I'll keep working on the prep work. Hopefully you'll make it back before I start the *actual* work, but if not, we'll get to see how difficult the recipe actually is for one person. And you'll have to try the results, no matter what they look like."

He studied her face. "You really don't mind."

"Ethan, it's your job. Would I love it if you're back before the cooking actually starts? Yes. Will I be upset if you're not? Absolutely not. If I lose my nerve and decide I don't want to tackle the recipe on my own, I'll pack the ingredients back up and make a sandwich and we'll try tomorrow. It's not a big deal."

"Okay." He kissed her cheek. He figured there was a ninety percent chance he'd be back within half an hour, but he didn't want to be wrong, so he said nothing. He jogged to his apartment and got the parts he was guessing he'd need, and his toolbox.

Luck—well, really it was more like experience—was on his side, and he let himself back into her apartment twenty-eight minutes later. He found her in the kitchen where he expected, humming along to the music on her phone, wiping down the counters. The ingredients were all in bowls of varying sizes, ready to go. She was so pretty, wearing leggings and a long sweater, fuzzy purple sock-like slippers, her hair pulled back into a bouncy ponytail.

She turned, sponge in hand, heading towards the sink, and spotted him. A simple smile of joy spread across her face and his heart just melted. Maybe his sister had been right all along. Maybe he hadn't been dating not because he was picky or because he was afraid of commitment, but because he simply hadn't met the right person.

Or he'd been waiting for her to come back home.

"You're back," she said, moving to rinse the sponge out, the happiness in her voice obvious.

"I am." He slid his arms around her, rubbing his lips lightly in her hair, pleased when she eased back into his body. She turned off the water, dried her hands and spun within the circle of his arms, coming up on her toes to kiss him. He really, really liked it when she did that.

"Mm. Still want to help me make dinner?" she asked.

"Definitely. You've done all the hard part. What needs to happen first?"

They worked together in an easy dance, taking turns reading the directions from the recipe out loud, stealing kisses now and again as the little kitchen heated up. When they sat down to eat, he poured the wine she'd opened and they clinked glasses.

"To us," he said.

Her grin slipped a little. "Is this... I've been wondering. What are we doing here?"

He drew in a quick breath. Really? After his conversation with Alyssa, he'd kept thinking about asking her about the lease, but he'd kept… Not. "We're being together."

"We said we didn't want commitment. Both of us said that."

"Are you not happy."

She frowned. "No, not at all. I mean, yes, I'm happy."

His heart had lurched at her 'no'. "But?"

"I—I don't know. We weren't doing that thing, but now we seem to be doing that thing."

"What would you like to be doing differently?"

"My lease will be up in three months," she said, not answering his question.

"But you haven't made any plans to leave." He tamped down on his instinct to get defensive. "And your lease can be extended quite easily. We're in a relationship, Rose. There's nothing wrong with that."

"We said friends with benefits. You said that's what you wanted."

He studied her. The fact that she sounded more panicked than angry helped keep him from overreacting. "And it was. But here we are. Why are you upset?"

"My mom asked me where I'm going to move to next."

He pursed his lips in thought. "I would have thought she'd be pushing you to stay."

"Yeah, me too," she grumbled.

"But that's beside the point. You haven't said anything about moving on. In the beginning, you mentioned researching cities, but you never brought it up again."

"I haven't had time. I've been busy. Seeing you and friends."

"Mm hm."

"You take up a lot of time, Ethan."

Her indignation set him off and he couldn't help but laugh.

She dropped her head in her hands, but at least she didn't bang it against the table.

"I don't want to leave," she said. At least, he thought that's what the muffled words said.

"Say that again," he requested, careful to keep the cheer out of his voice.

She sighed and lifted her head. "I was only supposed to stay for a little while, then go on my grand adventures around the world."

"What makes you think that can't happen? Was your timeline set in stone for some reason?"

Her face crumpled. "Because I'm so happy here. In Wildlife Ridge. With you."

He rubbed a hand over his face, partly to cover his smile, partly to scrub his brain into action and figure out what to say. He stood and grabbed her hand, pulled her over to the couch. He dropped down, giving her a tug so she landed in his lap.

When she curled into him, he relaxed.

"I'm glad you're happy, but you have a funny way of showing it," he said.

She snorted. "Sorry. I guess this has been running around in the back of my brain for a little while, but I've been refusing to actually think about it."

"Tell me."

"I was so proud of myself for reaching my goal. Having the freedom to go where I want, when I want, be able to work from anywhere. It was so important to me, and here I've reached it, and… I came home to my parents and met a man, so now my dream is dead."

His lips twitched at her dramatic tone, but she couldn't see them and he worked to keep the humor from his voice. "First of all, you can still go where you want, when you want, and work from anywhere. And you make it sound like you moved back into your mom's basement for free rent or something. That's not quite what you've done. I think you're surprised how much you like being in Wildlife Ridge."

"I am. I realized that, when I was thinking about traveling, *this* is what I was imagining. A small town where people know each other, take care of each other, where there's always something going on if you pay enough attention and participate. I just…figured there'd be less English."

This time he did chuckle, but she smiled as well, so he figured he was safe.

"I'm not asking you to sign a one-year lease or anything," he pointed out.

"What are you asking?"

CHAPTER SEVENTEEN

Rose forced herself to breathe. This wasn't a holding-your-breath conversation. She'd already made a fool of herself with her hysterics. Okay, well, it hadn't been that bad, and he wasn't freaking out about it. Instead, he'd snuggled her in close and asked her what was going on.

How had she gotten so lucky?

But she was still waiting for his response. She looked up, searched his face.

"I don't know what I'm asking. I can't—" He broke off, his eyes going shiny.

Rose rubbed a hand over his chest, her own heart aching.

"Alyssa—" he started, but then stopped again.

"I don't want to leave while she's holding on, either," Rose said. "Does that sound terrible? That I don't want to leave until she—"

His shook his head sharply. "It's okay. We have to be able to say it. We should be able to say it to each other. She's dying. And while she's here, I want to be here with her."

"Me too. I know it's not the same, but I want to be here for my friend, and I also want to be here for you."

"But if that makes you unhappy, putting off your travel—"

"No!" She put her hands on his cheeks, held his gaze. "That's not what it was about, at all. I promise."

When he nodded his understanding, she relaxed again. "It's all so muddled in my head, I guess. Like you said, I didn't expect to like being here so much, and being with you is so easy and amazing and I don't want it to end, and I'm just being silly, thinking that means I've given up on my dreams. But you're right, that's not true at all. I've reached my dream of being able to do what I want. I just don't seem to know what that is."

"Part of you is worried you're giving something up to be with a man."

"I guess. I don't want to be *that girl*."

"Later, after Alyssa…goes, if you still want, I would love to travel with you somewhere. Spend some time in different countries, compare some small towns to this one."

She was honestly shocked. "But…you never left. You love it here. Your job is here. You're such an amazing part of this community and what I love about it."

"I never left because at first I was taking care of Alyssa, then my mom, then I was getting my career going, then I was helping Alyssa and Jackson. But that's not a forever thing…and then there will be nothing holding me here, except for the fact that I like it. I do like living here, I'm not saying I don't. I don't know that I would want to travel around for the rest of my life. But I'd certainly be happy to try it for a while and see how it goes."

She squished up her face as she watched him, trying to understand. He wasn't going to turn out to be a Matt, was he? Like her friend Jennifer's loser husband? Sponging off his partner?

Not her Ethan. But, to so easily say he'd walk away from his job made her super uneasy. Maybe his inheritance had been more than she'd supposed?

"You realize you probably wouldn't be able to get work visas in most places? I suppose you could find some handyman work, under the table, but I don't know if it would—"

He laughed, cutting her off.

She frowned, seriously concerned. He'd seemed so responsible with money, had insisted he was saving for retirement. Maybe he didn't really understand the importance of continuing that? It was all about compound interest! Although he had seemed to get it.

He ran a finger over her forehead, forcing her to smooth out the wrinkles she'd formed trying to understand what he could be thinking. He was smiling, but it slowly faded, and he looked chagrinned. Confusion morphed to irritation and she narrowed her eyes at him.

"Um, shit. I can't believe this hasn't come up. I promise, the only reason is that I don't particularly like to talk about it. It's not that I was hiding it. I just get embarrassed," he said.

He was blushing, so she didn't doubt that part of it.

"I don't even know what we're talking about."

"My job. The way I make my money. Besides being a landlord, I mean."

"Wait. You own the building *and* you have an *entire job* that I don't know about? How is that possible."

He winced. "I mentioned my inheritance. I used that for the down payment on the building. And the other...I don't know. It's not a secret, like I said, I just find it embarrassing to talk about. I know Ian has called me Mr. Fix It in front of you. Nobody's mentioned YouTube to you? Really?"

She had wondered about his owning the building actually, so she let that go. But. "YouTube? Once or twice, I guess, but not about you, specifically. And sure, he's called you that, but you're the guy Erin calls to ask how to make her porch light run on a timer, or Ian calls to ask if he should get a new washing machine or have it repaired. Mr. Fix It."

He scrubbed his hand over his face and head.

"Yeah, well, I have a YouTube channel. If Erin mentioned learning about the light thing, it was on the channel, she didn't call me to ask about it."

Okay.

"You have a YouTube channel."

"And a podcast. And a blog. Between those and taking care of the building, I stay pretty busy. It's called DIY Fix It. Alyssa came up with the name and helped with a lot of the early stuff to help it get more popular. I didn't use my name, so she started signing stuff as Mr. Fix It. I thought it was silly, but she really got the early numbers rising fast. Now it's at the point where I don't really need to do anything except add content, since I'm not really worried about growing it further."

She stared at him. He stared back. It just…wasn't computing.

"I do one video a week and one podcast a week. I used to edit them, and my once-a-week schedule was a little sporadic some-times, but when Alyssa got sick I hired an editor. And I hired a virtual assistant to do a lot of what Alyssa did, handling the inter-view setups and requests, answering emails, responding to the comments and questions that aren't trolls. That kind of thing. With their help, now I'm consistent, video on Tuesday, podcast on Friday, and I have a couple of each banked in case I can't get the new content to the editor on time. "

He was rambling, and she still didn't know what to think. Virtual assistant? Editor? Interviews? "I don't really go on YouTube often, unless I'm searching for a recipe or something. You have, what, subscribers?"

He cleared his throat. "That's right."

"How many?"

He mumbled, but when she just raised her eyebrow at him, he repeated, "One hundred and thirteen thousand. Or so."

Wow. That sounded impressive. "And you make money doing this?"

"And the podcast. And the blog. The VA mostly handles the blog based on the video and podcast content. Ad revenue. Mostly it was a side gig, you know? All my money went to buying this building, maintaining and improving it. It makes decent money for me now, but at first it was tight, and every time there was a maintenance issue I was a little panicked. I tried to DIY as much as I could, and I found blogs, podcasts and channels to help me figure my way through it. Alyssa kind of pushed me into it, but I had fun doing it, so it stuck. People responded well, I learned more, was able to save more, invest more. But I still liked doing the DIY, and I liked the online community I'd joined, so I kept building that side of things, too."

"I'm blown away, to be honest."

"I hope you understand I wasn't intentionally keeping a secret. Exactly."

"No, I get it. And like you said, we weren't exactly communicating about where we were going with this whole thing. I was pretending to myself that my feelings weren't getting out of hand. That I could walk away when I was ready. Which is why I maybe lost my mind a little bit ago."

He kissed her, a quick relief that she wasn't mad at him, she could tell.

"But, I mean, how are you even doing this? I don't even remember seeing a computer at your place. And when?"

He blushed. "I keep the door to the second bedroom closed. I have a whole setup in there. Camera, mic. And, when you're working. Our schedules meshed pretty well, actually. It takes a few hours a day to do everything but the timing is flexible. Taking a break to fix someone's toilet or stopping to go help Alyssa, or whatever, isn't a big deal."

"Your place is two bedrooms?" she asked, astonished.

He laughed, and she couldn't help but join in.

"You sounded more surprised about the size of my apartment than my work."

"I might be," she agreed. "Wow. Okay. Anything else I should know about?" she teased.

"I want kids."

Her heart melted.

"I mean, not anytime soon. But I used to think I'd never want kids. Not more responsibilities. And—" He closed his eyes for a minute, breathed deeply. "The thought that they could get sick. I just...I didn't think I could risk that."

She rubbed his chest again, felt him relax under her hand.

"But now I realize how precious love is. I hate that we're losing Alyssa. I would give up my life for hers in a second. But to have never had her at all? That would have been a travesty. Not to know her light and spirit, her sweet and giving nature. Even when she was a bratty teenager, she was the best person I knew."

He wiped a tear that rolled down her cheek. "I hate that we're losing her," he repeated. "But I want kids, with *you*. I know it's super early to say that. Hell, an hour ago I was just hinting that I wanted a real relationship with you. And I do, but I want you to know that I see this going the distance, and I see us in a house with at least two kids. We don't have to commit to anything now, but that's my only other secret. That I see that for my future. For *our* future."

She sobbed into his chest, the happy and sad so huge within her that she couldn't speak, couldn't think, could only hang on to him as the emotions sorted themselves out. He let her cry, stroking her hair and murmuring soothing words in her ear as she brought it under control.

Finally, she sat up again. "This is why I was so confused. I couldn't see my future because it didn't make sense. Me, alone in Thailand or some tiny town in Spain or whatever. I couldn't see it anymore."

"Can you see it if I'm there with you?"

She nodded. "Yes. But I see our kids going to school here. I want to have adventures with you, and maybe we'll change our minds once we experience all the wonders out there, but right now, I can see us here, building a family, knowing we have the freedom to be who we want to be, where we want to be. We'll buy a house here and we can travel, but we'll have Wildlife Ridge to come home to whenever we want.

He hugged her tightly. "It's going to be hard, trying to plan for a future while also holding on to Alyssa. I might mess up again. Not tell you what I need to tell you, or say the wrong thing. I promise to try to be better about that, though."

"I was the same. All these thoughts running through my brain that I refused to acknowledge, so I didn't say anything to you. I'll do better about that."

"We're so adult."

She laughed and hugged him tight. "We totally are. Let's have ice cream."

CHAPTER EIGHTEEN

Rose accepted a kiss from Ethan and headed up to the roof. She'd run into Walter Anderson at the gas station earlier, and he'd told her he thought there would be an excellent sunset tonight. Ethan needed to catch up on some work, but he'd given her the key to the roof. She sat on the swing and realized that she should have brought up a glass of wine. Ah well, maybe they could come up later tonight with the wine, and watch the stars again.

She watched the movements of the town for a few minutes, marveling at the difference in her life in only a few months. Living in LA had been fun, she hadn't minded the hustle and bustle, the crowds of people. The traffic had sucked most of the time, sure, but it was just the thing that you put up with in order to live there. And she'd enjoyed living there. But it surprised her how much more she enjoyed living here.

The sun had sunk to the horizon and was beginning to fall below the line. She took out her phone and snapped a couple of pictures. She missed her girls, but they chatted regularly and were planning to come visit soon. There were clouds moving in and she was disappointed that they covered the top of the sun as it dipped below the horizon, so she didn't get that perfect last picture, but that was okay.

There would be more sunsets to come. She'd enjoyed going to Venice Beach every so often to catch the sunset there, and had far too many digital photos of those efforts.

Now, a hint of pink appeared in the offending clouds. Her phone rang and she glanced down to see it was Janelle.

"Hey, what's doing?"

"I tried this new healthy recipe using a Costco frozen salmon, and it was awful. I need to be distracted from the terrible memory."

Rose laughed. "I thought you said you were done with dieting. You know you don't need to."

"Done with dieting, yes, but trying to eat healthy in general."

"Okay, that's fair. Sorry about the salmon. We'll never speak of it again."

"Good. What are you doing?"

"I just watched the sun set."

"Time zones and the curvature of the earth are freaking weird. We won't have sunset for about forty minutes."

"Okay, yeah, that is weird."

As she was talking, the pink in the clouds was spreading and intensifying, edging more towards orange.

"Isn't Nay out on a date tonight?" she asked.

"Yeah, that financial planner. She thought if they're both passionate about finances, maybe it would give them a good connection."

"Maybe. Got to be better than your mom's chiropractor."

They both laughed at the disaster Janelle's date with Doug had been last month. The guy was clearly looking for a doormat, not a partner, and Janelle had not been there for that.

"I'm switching to video, you have to see this."

She did as she'd said and turned the phone to show Janelle how the orange had exploded across the sky, lighting up the clouds in a glorious display.

"Damn, that's impressive. I'd head to the beach to catch ours, but I think there's too much cloud cover tonight."

"Maybe we'll have some good sunsets while you're here."

"How's Ethan?"

"Oh, good, he pointed out to me that we're in a relationship and oh, by the way, he's an internet and podcast star."

"I'm sorry, what?"

Rose laughed. "We had a little discussion about the state of us last night. I had a bit of a freak out because we'd specifically said neither of us was looking for that."

"Looking doesn't mean not finding," Janelle said.

"Yeah, apparently. My brain wants to say no, that's not what we're doing, you can't just change on me, but then I realized it wasn't him changing, it was just understanding what we were already doing."

"Uh huh. I think I followed that."

"Anyway, he said that he'd like to have kids someday. With me."

"Uh, hello! We went from we're not just friends to let's have kids?"

"Well, there was a fair bit of conversation in between. And when we're talking, it all makes sense and when we're together it all makes sense, it's just later that I freak out a bit."

"Are you freaking out?"

"I'm wondering if it's all too fast and worried that it's happening at the same time I'm already making these huge life changes."

She turned the phone around again so that Nell could see how the color had deepened even further.

"Wow. Beautiful. I think you should stop overthinking things and just enjoy the fact that you're happy where you live, you're happy with your work and you're happy with your man."

"It's all kind of unbelievable."

"You worked hard to reach this point and it's completely okay to enjoy the results of that."

"Huh. You think?"

Janelle laughed. "Yes, I think."

Rose's phone beeped and she saw her mother was calling.

"My mom's calling so I'll let my wise guru go. Thanks."

"Thanks for sharing the beautiful."

Picking up her mom's call, Rose toed the ground so that the swing could do its thing.

"Hey, Mom."

"Hi, Rose. I got in a baking mood this afternoon and made brownies. I already dropped some off with your father and some with Belinda. If you take a few, I'll be left with a reasonable amount in the house and I'll be much happier."

"Gee, I guess I can do that for you," Rose said with a laugh.

"You're a good daughter. I'll be over in five minutes."

Smiling, she wondered how long it would take for Janelle to remember the bit about Ethan being a video and podcast star. She made sure the door was closed and locked behind her and went down to her floor. She wished she had some milk. She loved her mom's brownies best that way. Tea would have to do. She filled the electric kettle and turned it on and wondered if she should bring up the fact that her mom took brownies to her best friend, daughter and ex-husband. *What did that mean?* Deciding to not bring it up, she opened the door when her mom knocked.

"Hi sweetheart. Did you see the sunset? I should have told you to go outside."

"I did, it was pretty incredible."

Her mom went into the kitchen and nodded approvingly at the kettle that had just clicked off. She put the plate of brownies on the counter and peeled back the aluminum foil. "Let me know what you think, I made a little adjustment to the recipe."

Rose pulled down two small plates, but her mom waived her off, so she put one back. They poured two cups of tea and moved to the table.

"I ran into Lucy as I was coming in. She must be dating someone here?"

"I have no idea."

"Ever since she came back from her high school study abroad to France, she's been unbearable with that silly little accent."

"Ah, is that what happened? I had wondered. This brownie is delicious. I was a little worried when you said you'd made a change."

Beaming, her mother blew on her tea to cool it down a bit. "I thought they came out well." She looked around the apartment. "I'm surprised Ethan isn't here."

"He's doing some work but he'll probably be around later." She wasn't used to her mom having a view of her relationship with a man outside of what Rose told her on the phone, or who she introduced her to on visits. Well, probably time to bite the bullet and acknowledge that they were living in the same town now, so things were different. "We're seeing each other now."

"Well, I know that. Everyone knows that."

"Not really. Everyone knows what they think they see, but until last night, Ethan and I hadn't discussed being in a relationship. Now we have."

She knew she sounded a little bit pissy, but she couldn't help herself.

"You're in Wildlife Ridge now, Rose. People will talk. It's not about being mean."

Rose sighed. "I know. I'm sorry, I just...hadn't even come to terms with who we were to each other, but everyone was making their own assumptions."

"That's what people do. Doesn't matter if they're right or wrong."

"Mom...you've not always been a fan of Ethan's."

Her mom frowned. "He wasn't always very reliable, and he hasn't dated anyone in town in years. But I didn't want to say anything to you. You obviously didn't want to talk about him to me."

Rose kept her sigh to an internal one. "You...can be a bit judgmental," she pointed out.

The sniff her mother gave was part indignation, part admission of guilt.

"Does he make you happy?"

Rose didn't know why she was surprised at the question. "He does. I think...I really think I'm falling in love with him. It's so weird, because it's nothing like any other time I've thought that. But I can see myself being with him in twenty years. I can see him holding a child of ours on his shoulders while he walks down the street holding another kids hand."

"Then that's what matters. Whatever anyone in town thinks, even what I think, none of that has anything to do with your relationship. But, for what it's worth, people are happy for you both. I haven't always thought Ethan made the right choices. When he tossed away his scholarship to college, I was sure he'd just waste away his life. But he's been a rock to Alyssa through her battles. And I may have held a bit of a grudge that he broke my baby's heart."

Rose put her hand on her mom's arm. "Thanks, mom. He had good reason, but I appreciate you being on my side."

"Always."

"I'm really worried about Alyssa," Rose said, softly.

"No, Rose, we're not thinking like that. Alyssa is fighting. Ethan and Jackson are fighting for her. The town is supporting her. She will win this fight. Alyssa has to believe that. We all have to believe that."

The tremble in her mom's voice had Rose reaching out to touch her arm. "Okay, Mom."

She tried to think of another direction to take the conversation in, but wasn't sure her mom would be any happier with the other topic that was on her mind. "Did you…You don't have to talk about this if you don't want to, but I was wondering. When you decided to marry Dad, you were in love and you thought it would last forever. When you look back now, do you regret it?"

"No, never. How could I, when it brought me you? But even outside of that, we loved each other very much and I would never wish that away." She shook her head, drank some tea. "I probably said differently, during the divorce. And I'm sorry for how that hurt you."

"No, Mom, that's not what I was trying to say."

"I know, but I am sorry. I only hurt so much at the time because we loved each other so much. I thought we would go through every phase of our lives together. Looking back, we could have made it work. There was enough love there, if we hadn't both been idiots. I regret the things I said, and the things I didn't say. But I don't regret falling in love, getting married, having you."

"I'm glad. I guess the hard part is that in all of my planning for the future these last few years, I've been imagining my ideal life, and I only had the most vague ideas about a husband and kids. I thought I wanted that, but I couldn't fit anyone into that picture, and now it's so easy to see Ethan there that it's scary."

"It's okay to be a little bit scared, as long as you don't turn your back on the possibilities."

"Thanks, Mom."

Rose decided she deserved a second brownie and, without asking, she brought one for her mom as well.

"I know I don't understand your work, Rose, and your father told me you were annoyed with me for that."

"Oh. Well, not annoyed that you don't understand it, but annoyed that you don't believe me when I tell you it's going really well. I have satisfied clients, excellent referrals and I'm already thinking of raising my prices. I thought you'd be excited for me, working for myself, making a success of my business."

"I am. I'm just old fashioned enough that I expect to be able to see and understand a business. I like computers, but I don't really understand making money on them. Like Ethan with his videos. I always figured it was more for fun than for work, but Pam tells me he really does quite well with that."

"Mom. Were you checking up on Ethan's potential as a husband?"

Her mom didn't even pretend to look abashed. "Of course I was."

This time Rose sighed out loud. "I'm thirty-four."

"And?"

Rose couldn't help but laugh and shake her head. "All right. Well, I'll give you that if you'll just promise to believe me when I tell you that my business is going really well, as is Ethan's, so there's no need to try and offer us jobs."

"Ah. Well. Yes, your father did make that point to me when you first came back. About you, I mean, we weren't talking about Ethan then. And I'm very proud of what you've accomplished, now that you've explained a little better. But, Rose, did you really hate working at the store?"

"No, I enjoyed working there in high school."

"You started talking about going to UCLA when you were twelve. I thought you just wanted to get out of the small town, but now you're back, so maybe it was the work you didn't like?"

"I wanted to go learn computer programming." Rose pushed her empty plate back and picked up her tea. "And yes, I wanted to be in a place where I could go to the movies without having to drive for an hour, where I could see a concert without planning an overnight trip. Where I could meet boys that I hadn't known since kindergarten and where the whole town wouldn't know and be talking about the fact that my date had to cancel at the last minute for prom. None of it had anything to do with the store. Or you or dad."

"When you left, I didn't think you'd be back. So I gave up on the idea of you ever taking over the store. My father's store. But when you said you were coming back, even if just for a while, I started to think about that again. I didn't want to scare you off with the idea of it, though."

"Oh. Wow. I never even thought about that. Which is kind of stupid, I realize now."

"I wanted you to work in the store for fun money, but your father and I were careful to never make the store an obligation for you. If we couldn't run it successfully without the help of a teenager, we figured it wasn't meant to be."

"You were forced to work in the store when you were growing up."

Her mother fiddled with her tea cup then nodded. "My father wanted a son. But my mother had two miscarriages after I was born, so he was stuck with me. He told me from an early age that I would need to get married so he could pass the store on to my husband."

"Oh, ouch. That is not cool, at all."

"It was a different time."

"Still."

"Yes. But the thing was, I loved the store. And I wanted to get married and run it. So there was no need to fight with him about any of it. But I wanted to."

Rose snorted. "Of course you did. I'm glad you did. But also glad that you wanted the store."

"We talked about it, before we got married. I told your father that if our children wanted the legacy, then we would pass it on, but I never wanted them to have the expectation that their life plan was already mapped out for them, before they were even born."

"Well, you did a good job of that."

"I'm glad."

"I would be proud to own your store someday, even if I have a manager run it instead of me or my husband. And I would spend time behind the counter, regardless. It's a legacy I'm proud of."

"Good. I'm glad. But your father and I aren't leaving any time soon."

Rose kissed her cheek. "Good. Thanks for the brownies. I'll see if I can manage to save one for Ethan."

"I'll bring extras next time."

Rose saw her out. While she put the plate and mugs in the dishwasher, it occurred to her that she'd had more meaningful conversations with her mom since she'd been back than she'd had the entire time she'd been in Los Angeles. And she was glad for it.

CHAPTER NINETEEN

Rose squeezed Ethan's hand in excitement when she finally saw Naomi and Janelle emerge from the airport hallway and into the baggage claim area. She ran to hug her friends, and introduced Janelle to Ethan. He waited patiently as they chattered at a hundred miles an hour, as if they hadn't been on the phone together just last night. But it was different seeing them in person, and she knew he understood that.

When she leaned back into him, he put an arm around her waist, and she saw Janelle and Naomi exchange smiles. It had been a month since Rose had told them she and Ethan were officially in a relationship. Naomi had claimed she'd known they would be together since the first night at Wolfhound Tavern, and Rose didn't argue with her about it.

Their two suitcases were finally spotted and wrangled and they piled into her car. She'd accepted his offer to drive back so she'd be able to talk more easily without having to watch the road.

"Oh," she cried, turning in her seat to face them. "I get to tell you news, because you were flying when Jennifer called me, and she told me I could fill you in." She turned to Ethan. "Jennifer is the one whose husband lost his job and became a loser who refused to get off his ass and do anything."

"You said she got remarried a while back, right?" he asked.

"Yes, three years ago, to Brad. We love Brad, they make a great pair."

"Okay, cool."

She turned back around. "They're pregnant!"

Janelle promptly pulled out her phone and dialed Jennifer on speaker so they could congratulate her. Rose glanced over at Ethan, loving the little smile on his face as he listened to them gush over the news. Brad sounded prouder than a peacock, while Jennifer was amused and excited.

By the time they hung up the phone, they were halfway to Wildlife Ridge and Rose was getting a little hungry. "How about we stop off at BBQ and Taphouse for dinner when we hit town?" she asked. "I haven't had a burger in over a month. It's a travesty."

"Works for me—" Naomi started to say.

"I was thinking with you ladies together for the first time since Rose left LA, that's more of a celebration, and deserves Monarch for dinner," Ethan interrupted.

"That's the fancy place," Naomi told Janelle.

"I can get a burger some other time," Rose agreed.

"Speaking of fancy places," Janelle said, and launched into a story about her boss, Tony the Asshole, and a reservation mishap that had them all laughing hysterically.

"Nell, how much longer are you going to put up with this crazy?" Rose asked.

"It mostly doesn't bother me. I mean, that was funny as hell and didn't affect my work. But the market's been good to me, and I'm actually ahead of my projections, so…I really could quit in a year or so. Depends on how much cushion I want."

"Which really means you could quit today, because you'll probably start working at least part time right away, doing something you actually like, anyway."

"Basically, yeah. But I'll feel better if I hit my number, and I'm not that unhappy. I find that the closer I get to my goal, the more real it is, the less I care about the bullshit at work. It just doesn't bother me like it used to."

"Because you know you could quit at any second, if you really wanted to," Naomi guessed.

"Probably. I mean, I still want to leave, but I'm more calm about it now and thinking about how to coordinate my future, more than what's wrong with my present. Now I'm ready to start researching places to live. I couldn't see past the present enough to do that before."

"Well, that is definitely progress," Naomi said, and high-fived her.

"Speaking of research," Janelle said, "have you guys made any decisions?"

"We've made progress," Rose said.

Ethan snorted.

"We have!" She laughed, though, because she knew he was right. "Okay, so, the truth is, we've narrowed it down to Europe."

"Well," Janelle said slowly. "I guess that's progress. I mean, two weeks ago you were at Asia, South America or Europe, so...sure. Progress."

Ethan laughed and Rose playfully slapped his shoulder.

"It so hard," she said. "When you can choose to go anywhere you want, when your only criteria is that it doesn't have a high cost of living but decent internet, the choices are nearly endless."

"But isn't there anywhere you've always wanted to go?" Naomi asked.

"Yes. France. Spain. Ireland. Scotland. Thailand. Japan. Honduras. Guatemala. Italy. England. Vietnam—"

"Okay, okay," Naomi said. "I get it. But remember, it's not like you only get to pick once. You just have to pick first."

"Easy for you to say," Ethan said.

"I guess."

"Seriously, Nay, don't tell me you couldn't move pretty much anywhere in the world you wanted right now," Rose said. "If you really wanted to, you could make it happen."

"You're not wrong," Naomi agreed.

"It's so hard," she whined, but smiling as she did so.

Ethan reached over and took her hand. "We'll figure it out. Or we'll make a long list, put each option in a bowl, and pick one out."

"Yes! I love that idea. We'll totally do that. I'll start the list next week."

She lifted his hand and kissed it, then turned back around to find her friends smiling at her with goofy grins.

As they neared town, she decided she wasn't too hungry to change the plans a bit. "How about you drive us home so we can change into fancier, cuter outfits, since we're going to the nice restaurant?"

"Agreed," Naomi said.

"Yes, that," Janelle said.

"You got it," Ethan said. "While you're getting ready, I'll call and see if it's busy."

Forty-five minutes later, they walked into the restaurant and people turned to stare. Rose wasn't surprised. Ethan looked hot in his slacks and the slate-blue, open-collared shirt she'd gotten him for his birthday the previous week. Naomi was rocking knee-high boots and a bronze wraparound dress that looked amazing on her. And Janelle was kicking up her height in stiletto booties that looked killer with her sweater dress. Ethan had seemed to appreciate her floral print maxi dress, though she'd had to bring a wrap to cover her shoulders as it was still cool out.

Basically, they looked amazing.

They were seated quickly and Ethan introduced them to their waiter, Ruben.

"Ruben and his parents moved here about ten years ago," Ethan said. "He's finished college and learning the hospitality industry."

"I want to own a place like this," Ruben said, flushing as he couldn't seem to stop looking at Janelle.

"Then I'm sure you will," Nell said, giving him a smile of encouragement that Rose was pretty sure had Ruben losing the power of speech.

"Okay, Ruben, we'll take a look at the menus, thanks," Ethan said, laughter in his voice. He clapped Ruben on the arm and gave him a tiny shove to get him moving.

Janelle was oblivious, and Naomi stifled a smile.

ETHAN WOULDN'T FORGET the dinner at Monarch anytime soon. The ladies were hilarious together, and he was incredibly charmed by all three of them. He already loved Rose, had thought he'd seen all sides of her, but as part of this group, she had a specific wit he hadn't seen yet, and a rapport that was just adorable to witness.

He dropped them off at home, appreciating that they still had both apartments. He and Rose had already discussed that when her lease was up, she'd move in with him and she hadn't freaked out when he'd mentioned buying an older place to renovate and move into, eventually.

It was a quick trip to Alyssa's house. When he went inside, he found that Alyssa had taken a long nap and was having a good day. She was so full of energy that he asked if she wanted Rose to come over with her friends. His sister's instant excitement told him the answer, and he called Rose.

"We are so in for that," she said immediately. "And we're not even going to bother changing, which means we're driving, 'cause cute shoes, so we'll be there in five minutes. Should we bring anything?"

"No. If you want, we can throw some cheese on a plate and crack open a bottle of wine."

"Sold."

Alyssa decided that if the ladies were dressed up, she would be too, so Jackson took her back into the bedroom. When the doorbell rang, Alyssa was coming down the hall in a pretty dress and a colorful scarf on her head. He got that damn lump in his throat, but it was quickly extinguished by the excited chatter all around him.

They settled into the living room—declining the offer of cheese and wine, as they were still too full from dinner—and he was amazed to watch as the trio of women folded Alyssa into their pack with ease and complete sincerity. They occasionally lassoed him or Jackson into the conversation, but for the most part, he and his brother-in-law just sat back and enjoyed the show.

Last week, her doctor had mentioned hospice care. They knew it was coming. Soon. But she still had days like today, and they were such a gift. Two weeks ago, Pam had brought some friends over and they'd done the whole manicure-pedicure thing. Alyssa had laughed telling him about it later, after she'd rested.

But he knew. Jackson knew. If she wasn't ready for hospice care, he'd look into having someone come in once a day for a couple of hours, to help out as needed, even if that just meant keeping Alyssa company or making dinner.

After an hour, he could see Alyssa start to flag. He didn't have to say a word. Janelle gave a delicate yawn and apologized, blaming their travel for her need to head out. Rose and Naomi were immediately in line, and they were all out the door within five minutes. He spoke to Alyssa for a few minutes, sharing his plans for the immediate future, then headed out.

Ethan went home and got to work. He expected the ladies to chat well into the night, since this was the first time they'd seen each other in person for months. He wouldn't even be surprised if Rose slept up there, but he was going to be prepared, either way.

He texted Rose and told her that he was going to be working on some video stuff, so to please text him when she was coming down so he could hit pause and save before she made any noise at the door. She didn't think to question the fact that he'd never asked that of her before.

He carried his supplies up to the roof, careful not to make any noise on the stairs. It was nearly ten now, so unless there was a real emergency, no one was likely to call or text him, but if they heard him out and about, they might flag him down.

Most of the work he'd wanted to do on the porch swing was

already done, so he only needed a half hour to finish that up. He made sure his phone was well charged, and double-checked the items in the storage bin, even though he knew it was all there.

Okay, he was set. He was prepared to go with the flow. If she stayed upstairs until super late, or even all night, he had a plan. If she came home now, he was ready. He just needed…her.

He tried to lose himself in his work, but was too easily distracted, so he turned on the television. When his phone beeped that she was coming down, just after eleven, he couldn't have said what he was actually watching. Some kind of sports highlights. Or something. It didn't matter.

It was time.

When she opened the door to the hallway, he was waiting for her. Her surprise was clear on her face, mostly because she'd expected him to be in the apartment, but also, he guessed, because he was still wearing his dinner clothes. So was she, though she was carrying her shoes in one hand.

"Want to go up to the roof for a little bit, or are you too tired?" he asked.

Her smile was the sweetest gift.

"That would be nice. Probably not for long, though. I'm super glad we prepped the breakfast stuff before we went to the airport. That was smart of you to suggest."

"I'm full of smart ideas."

"Don't I know it," she said as she led the way up the stairs. She stopped at the top to slip her shoes back on.

He pulled his phone from his pocket and triggered the lights, using the app he'd already cued up. A quick switch of apps had the Bluetooth speaker starting, so when Rose opened the door, she caught her breath.

Easing up to the step behind her, he peaked over her shoulder.

There was now a gazebo surrounding the swing, with more lights. The music was just loud enough to be heard from where they stood, but she probably couldn't quite make out the song.

He took her hand and eased past her, pulling her along behind him until she made it to the seat. She sat and watched him silently as he opened the chest and pulled out a blanket. It was a different one than she was used to seeing, blue with silver stars shooting across it. He leaned over and kissed her, then stepped back and held up the blanket so she could see it.

Across the stars, in silver threads, it read *Will you marry me?*

She gasped, and he dropped the blanket low enough so he could see her face. Her hands covered her mouth. He placed the blanket around her, pulled the box from his pocket, and dropped to his knees in front of her.

"I never thought I'd be here, asking someone to share their life with me, to make room for me on their journey, wherever that may lead. I don't care where we are. As long as we're together, I know that I'll be home. If you take a chance with me, I will spend the rest of my life doing my best to support you however you need, encourage you in all that you do and love you with all that I am. Will you marry me?"

She bypassed the ring he was holding out for her, throwing her arms around him. "Yes! Oh Ethan, I want to share my life with you!"

"Well, then, put the ring on." He chuckled. "Unless you don't like it?"

Pulling back, she reached for the box.

"Oh, it's so beautiful, Ethan."

Her hand shook a little as he took the delicate, antique-looking gold ring out of the box and slid it onto her finger. He'd gone for a slightly smaller diamond than he'd originally looked at, partly because she had delicate fingers, but also thinking ahead that in some of the locations they would be living, subtle would be better.

"I love it; it's amazing. I love you." She kissed him, but pulled back quickly. "Oh, I want to shout up here, but I won't. I also want to call the girls, but not yet."

He sat down next to her and she immediately shared the blanket. He reached into the bin and pulled out champagne and two glasses. "There are two more glasses, if you want to call them up to the roof, or we can take them down whenever you're ready."

She had tears in her eyes as she accepted the flute of bubbly. "You would share your roof with my friends?" she asked.

"I think I can trust them not to give away our secret."

"Let's just look at the stars for a few minutes, and enjoy the champagne." She leaned into him, his arm automatically going around her shoulders and pulling her in.

"Is this crazy?" she asked softly. "We've only re-known each other four months."

"Maybe it's crazy, but I have no doubts. We can wait as long as you want, though."

"No, I don't want to wait. We'll start planning right away." She turned her face up to his. "I love you."

He kissed her for a long moment. Then she pulled back, a puzzled look on her face. "Has that same song been playing the whole time?" she asked.

Laughing, he pulled out his phone and turned off the repeat feature, letting Kelly Clarkson fade off at the end of the song. Then Rose was on her phone, and he leaned over to see what she texted.

TAKE THE STAIRS UP TO THE ROOFTOP. NOW!!! (Please)

Soon, they were all crying and hugging and oohing and awing, and he sent Alyssa a picture of the ring on Rose's finger to indicate that the proposal he'd told her about had been a success.

"I'm so glad I'm wearing a pretty dress," Rose said, laughing as Naomi took their picture. "You planned well." She lifted her face for another kiss, and he was happy to oblige.

When they finally made it to the bedroom, she posed for him wearing nothing but the ring, then she pounced on him.

He'd thought his heart couldn't get any fuller, but she proved him wrong. Her touch, her words, her trust, she gave him everything, and he tucked it all into his heart for safekeeping, and understood that would always expand, there would always be room for everything she was, inside of him.

"Always," she whispered, as if she'd heard him.

"Always," he repeated.

EPILOGUE

Rose watched Ethan from a few feet back, as he knelt on the ground where Alyssa had been laid to rest. There was no marker yet. It had only been a week since she'd finally ended her long fight. Three days since they'd put her in the ground. Rose had stood by his side then, holding his hand, crying but no longer sobbing. There had been plenty of that as she and Ethan held on to each other over the past several days. Weeks, really.

It was twelve weeks since Alyssa had been put on hospice care. Eighteen weeks since Rose had accepted Ethan's proposal.

It had all gone so quickly. Alyssa had been beyond excited for them, and her pride at having helped Ethan pick out the beautiful ring had been extremely sweet. She loved her brother, and had no reservations about enfolding Rose into that love. When she had thanked Rose, thanked her for loving Ethan, Rose hadn't been able to hold back her tears. Alyssa had soothed her, told her she was proud to become Rose's sister.

In six months, Rose would marry Ethan, without his sister there to witness. But that wouldn't keep Rose from referring to the woman as her sister for the rest of her life. After the wedding, they would leave Wildlife Ridge. For a while. But they would be back.

Ethan was right, home would be wherever they were, together, but this town was in their hearts and always would be.

But today was the day Ethan was going to say goodbye, she knew. At the funeral and burial, there'd been too many people, he'd told her. He'd appreciated them, all who had come to mourn Alyssa's passing, and to celebrate her life.

"That was important. Jackson needed that. I needed that," he'd told her. "But after everyone's gone, I need a little quiet time to say goodbye."

They'd taken Jackson to the airport yesterday. He was going to spend a week in Oregon with his parents before coming back to take over as manager of Ethan's apartment buildings. He'd quit his job at the grocery store last month, needing to spend those final weeks with Alyssa, a move that Ethan and Rose had fully supported.

Ethan stood and she waited for him. When he turned, she let out a long, shaky breath. He was smiling. Blinking back tears, she reached for his hand when he made it to her, but he ignored her and enfolded her in a hug.

"I'm okay," he said. "I can feel her now, in my heart. It was too much before, too heavy. I couldn't talk to her."

Rose nodded her head against his chest.

"It still hurts, a whole fucking lot, but I can talk to her again. I was afraid I wouldn't be able to. Wouldn't be able to tell her about our wedding, or Spain, or...our kids."

She just nodded again. No way could she get words past the lump in her throat. They'd asked Alyssa to do the honors of picking a country from the bowl, and she'd been thrilled. She'd helped them make wedding plans and research Spanish cities, knowing all along that she wouldn't be there for the wedding, wouldn't be able to wave them off on their journey.

They'd considered a rush wedding, but Alyssa had vetoed that. She wanted them to plan everything out properly, and to help with it.

"This wedding isn't about me," she'd told Rose. "I don't want it to turn into that. I don't want my sick body to be the focus on your day. Don't ever doubt that I will be there, watching over you, in spirit. Besides, the day itself isn't the main thing. Seeing you together, in love, so happy, that's all I need."

Rose had protested that it wouldn't be like that, but Alyssa had been firm and Rose had stopped arguing and started planning. At first, some part of her had hoped that it would give Alyssa something to hold on for, a reason to keep fighting, but that had been foolish. In six months, she would walk down the aisle to Ethan, and she would know that Alyssa had been part of making the day wonderful. And she would be present, in their hearts.

Ethan turned her towards his truck. "I'm going to call the caterer and see if they can do something with figs for the tasting."

"Figs?"

"Do you hate them?"

"I have no strong feelings about them."

"Good, we'll see what they do."

"You've been watching cooking shows on YouTube again, haven't you?" She said it teasingly, but her heart was leaping. They hadn't had any conversations about the wedding since Alyssa had passed. She just hadn't been able to think past the next few hours, then the next few days, and knew he'd been the same.

He grinned at her as they got into the car. "Maybe. Let's get sushi," he suggested.

She laughed and agreed. Her man was starting to heal. A short road trip to go get some sushi seemed like a fine idea to her.

They talked about wedding plans, the merits of the three cities they'd narrowed things down to in Spain, Alyssa, Jackson, Naomi's decision to stop dating for a while, and Nell's plan to fix up and sell an old Porsche she'd found.

When they made it back to town after dinner, she was surprised when he turned off before their street, but didn't say anything. And began to smile as he wound his way back behind the town proper and into the more deserted streets. Finally, he pulled into a turnout and shut off the truck.

"The problem with these newer vehicles is that the lights don't go off when you turn the truck off," he said with a grin.

Laughing, she unbuckled her seat belt and scooted closer.

"What were you thinking of doing, out here in the dark?"

"I'm thinking all kinds of things." He unbuckled as well, and turned to her. He leaned in and brushed his lips over hers. "All kinds of wicked things."

She sighed. "I like the way you think."

EXCERPT

Breaking Free
(Fully Invested Book 2)
By KB Alan
(Available now)

When Janelle comes to Wildlife Ridge for her best friend's wedding, she's not expecting to fall for the little town. Or it's newest resident. But Aaron Romero is full of charm once he comes out of hiding and he's set his eyes on Nell.

Aaron's happy in his new home, working on his art and ignoring the town outside his gate. Until his car breaks down and Janelle and her grandmother stroll over for the rescue. Now he can't get her out of his mind and he's willing to brave the whole town and a wedding to see where things might lead.

CHAPTER ONE

When Janelle had been told her best friend Rose's wedding would be in mid-April, she'd foolishly assumed that meant a decently warm, sunny day. The fact that she'd spent most of her life in California, with frequent trips to family in Hawaii, had clearly skewed her perspective on April weather.

No matter how much she checked her weather app as she packed for her trip to Wildlife Ridge, Colorado, her brain had a hard time accepting that she needed to be prepared for rain, snow, *and* sun. Giving in to the inevitable, she called her mom and asked if she could borrow her parents' big suitcase. A wedding event wasn't the time to not have the right clothes, and Wildlife Ridge didn't have any clothes shops that she could recall. It was a charming and tiny town, and she was looking forward to returning, but she wasn't planning a shopping spree.

She checked her watch. Her parents lived in Westwood, less than five miles from her house. If she tried to make the drive during commute times, it would take about forty minutes. But right now, on a Saturday afternoon, she bet herself ten dollars that she could do it in fifteen.

Grabbing her purse, she locked up her guesthouse and walked the half block to her car. She liked her little rental, but the one thing she would change, if it wasn't stupid expensive to do so, was her lack of a parking spot.

Weaving in and out of traffic with the ease of someone born and raised in Los Angeles, she quickly pulled into her parents' driveway and checked her watch. Fourteen minutes.

"Yes!"

She pulled out her phone and made an entry in her budgeting app, pulling ten dollars from her discretionary category and moving it into her treats category. Then she frowned. The stupid category was up to one hundred and eighty dollars.

She had a…well, could you call it a bad habit? Maybe. She had a habit of letting the treats category fill up and not actually treating herself to anything. Now that Rose had moved away, she and Naomi had fewer excuses to celebrate with dinner at a nice restaurant. She made a mental note to decide on something special for herself once she got home from the wedding weekend.

When she walked into the house, she smelled incense and stuck her head around the corner into the den. Her parents were there, in front of the open butsudan, eyes closed, chanting.

While she'd fallen out of the Buddhist habits she'd been raised with, seeing her parents in their peaceful moment made her happy and a bit nostalgic. They'd had the same butsudan, the alter where they kept the gohonzon and offerings, since she was a kid, and the same routine. Plus, it meant that they'd also bet she'd be at least twenty minutes in her drive, giving them enough time to go through their process, and they had lost.

Grinning, she jogged up the stairs. When she got to the top, she stopped, turned round, went back down, turned around, and jogged back up, panting a bit as she reached the top. She'd read this was a good exercise technique for people who didn't want to specifically plan a time in their day for working out. Every time she encountered stairs, she was supposed to do them twice.

So far, she had discovered that there were actually very few staircases in her day-to-day environment. Who knew?

She pulled the suitcase out of the closet and headed back down. Was it cheating to leave the suitcase at the bottom on her return trip up? There hadn't been a rule about what she was carrying. Panting more substantially by the time she got back up, she turned and walked down, smiling at her parents as they stepped out of the study.

They exchanged hugs and moved to the living room to chat.

"I'm sorry I missed dinner last night, my boss decided to go to Mumbai and it was a bit of a scramble at the last minute."

Her mother frowned. "That boss of yours."

"True, but I got a raise last week, so I can live with his bad time management for a little longer. And, this means he'll be otherwise occupied for at least a few days while I'm in Colorado."

"That's good. Your grandmother is excited to be joining you."

"Rose loves her, and it'll be fun to have her there. And I know she's really looking forward to going to the war memorial in Denver."

"Honey, are you sure you don't want a ride to the airport?" her father asked.

"Thanks, Dad, but no reason to drag you out to LAX. The company has a contract with a valet service. It's one of the few company perks that I can actually use once in a while."

Her dad's lips twitched. "Getting fancy on us."

She rolled her eyes at him. "Yeah, that's me, next thing you know I'll be ordering a car service and sipping champagne while they drive me to my chartered jet."

He leaned in and kissed her cheek. "Go big, buy the jet yourself."

Laughing, she hugged them both again and headed out.

With the larger suitcase, packing was much easier. She just threw in two-thirds of her closet and called it done. She ate a light dinner and set her alarm. She needed to be at the airport earlier than normal in order to meet her grandmother's arrival. They would have time for lunch before catching the flight to Denver.

The drive to the valet service was easy, and she only had to pause at the curb for a moment as the driver jumped into her passenger seat. She gave the young man her company's corporate info as she drove the rest of the way to the airport, and he filled out the form on his tablet. He was out of the car and waiting for her to pop the trunk by the time she'd shifted into park and detached her car key from the rest.

He had her suitcase on the curb and her receipt ready for her by the time she's made it to the back of the car. Nice and smooth. She hoped the rest of her trip managed to go so well.

Three hours later, she and Grandma were settled into their seats and ready to go. She texted the update to Rose, who responded with a series of emojis that made Grandma laugh.

"How come you didn't fly out at the same time as Naomi?"

Naomi, third best friend in her and Rose's trio, had left two days earlier. "She was going to travel around and scout some rental properties she's thinking of buying."

Janelle didn't add that she hadn't been about to let Grandma make the full flight from Hawaii to Denver on her own when it was simple enough to coordinate the layover with her own flight from Los Angeles.

"I'm just amazed at what that girl has accomplished. How many buildings does she have now?"

"She has the triplex she started with, the one you visited. She moved out of that two years ago and bought a four-unit building, but so far that's it. She's decided that it's silly to only invest in Los Angeles when she can get so much more for her money in other markets, so that's what she's looking at now. She liked Colorado when she was visiting Rose and figured she might as well look around. She has the money ready to invest somewhere cheaper, now, or she'd have to wait another year to be able to invest here."

"Smart girl. I'm so proud of all of you, making your way on your own, not waiting for a man to get your life started."

The plane started to taxi and Janelle held her grandmother's hand. "Do you regret marrying Grandad so young?"

Grandma pursed her lips. "No, but it's a different time now. I worried about your mother when she followed suit and married even younger than me. But that girl met your father and knew what she wanted and wasn't going to waste any time getting it."

"She had me when she was only twenty."

"They were here in California by then, and she told me the only time she got weird looks was when her hands were swollen in pregnancy and she had to take off her wedding ring."

"That, and people asking her if she was the nanny when she would take me to the park."

Grandma looked at her solemnly. "She told you that?"

Nell gave her a wry smile. "She said I was a super-white baby, didn't start getting my color until later. And there weren't many other half-Japanese, half-Hawaiian natives in the neighborhood."

"She told me she hoped California would be more progressive with a mixed marriage, but sometimes she wondered if she should have talked your dad into going back to Canada. But…"

Nell and her grandmother grinned at each other as they both mock shivered. "Cold," Nell agreed. "And here we are, heading to Colorado. Have you ever been to the mountains?"

"Your grandfather and I took the kids to Park City, Utah, when they were in high school. Your uncle begged and begged for the chance to learn how to ski, and the girls said they would try as well. He took a couple of lessons and did okay, but he never asked again. Your mom did fairly well, and your Aunt Linda was too busy flirting with all the boys to give it a proper try."

Nell grinned again at her grandmother as the flight attendant came by to offer them drinks. They relaxed and chatted for a while, until a nicely muscled Latino man moved down the aisle towards them, presumably on his way to the bathroom.

Grandma nudged Janelle's arm. "You haven't told me about any dates lately. You could go stand in line for the restroom, you'll have a few minutes to chat, see what he's like."

"Ah, come on, don't you have enough grandkids by now?"

Grandma put her hand on Nell's arm. "It's not that, my darling. It's that I want to see you happy."

"I *am* happy. And maybe I'll get married and have kids, maybe I won't. But I promise you, I'll be happy either way. I enjoy my life. Dating is fun. But I haven't met anyone that…I don't know, makes me excited to see them after the first date."

"No quiver in your loins?"

"Grandma!" Nell laughed. "I mean, I'm not saying I'm not having fun now and then, but no, I haven't found anyone who makes my loins quiver with excitement at the idea of seeing them."

Grandma frowned. "But you're happy? Working a job you don't like, playing with cars in your spare time, and having occasional fun with dates?"

"It's not my job I don't like, just my boss. The work is fun. And the cars are fun. I sold that Porsche I fixed up for a nice profit, and I had a great time doing the work. I know I'm thirty-six and you already had all three of your kids by my age—"

"No, don't go by that, it was a whole different world for women. My mother got married at the end of the war, and she was twenty; her parents were afraid she was already too old. But she insisted on waiting for my father to come home."

"And you got married at twenty, too. Did you think you were getting too old?"

"No, I just felt ready."

"And you found a Hawaiian boy, who wasn't Japanese. Were you worried about bringing him home?"

Grandma smiled, her gaze going fuzzy with memory. "No, it might have been different if it hadn't been for the war, but after…I guess they didn't hold on to many of the old traditions. I can't even speak Japanese anymore. I wanted my children to learn, but it wasn't taught in the school, and I didn't know it well enough. I tried to get my mother to speak it to them, but it didn't really take. I'm glad your father taught you his French."

"Me, too. And mom followed tradition and got married at twenty."

"She was ready to get off the island. Which was funny, because your father wanted to stay."

"And surf."

Grandma laughed. "Yes, and surf. That's why he'd come, after all. But your mother was smart enough to know he wouldn't want to stay forever, and once he was ready to go, she would have her chance."

"Couldn't she have gone away for college?"

"Yes, but—and you must never tell her I told you this—she was too afraid to go off on her own. She didn't have your independence. With your father at her side, she was ready to dare anything. But on her own, she would not have left the island. At least not for several years."

"That's okay, she made it work."

"She did, yes, and he was a good match for my oldest. He lets her be brave, and she not only gives him family, but the need for family."

"Yeah, his parents weren't nearly as awesome as you and Grandpa."

"Well. Few are."

Janelle laughed. "And at least two of my cousins upheld the tradition of marriage at twenty."

"Ah, those two. They both should have waited. Maybe not as long as you, though."

Grandma's phone beeped and she picked it up to check the message. Janelle leaned over as she sighed.

"What now?"

"Your aunt received koden from her old neighbor and she's deciding how many stamps to send in the thank you card."

Janelle's aunt's father-in-law had passed away several weeks before. The Japanese had a tradition of sending money to grieving families when they experienced a loss. For reasons that weren't clear to Janelle, Japanese American families on the mainland had then added to the tradition by sending postage stamps in their thank you cards. The number of stamps was determined by how much money had been sent. That amount of money was also important, to avoid giving insult. Grandma Yuki had a list of how much she'd sent, who she'd sent it to, how much she'd received, whose loss she'd received it for, and the corresponding number of stamps. Janelle found the whole thing fascinating, but was kind of hoping it would die off with her generation.

"Sometimes I wish this stamp tradition had been kept to the mainland," Grandma grumbled as she waited for her daughter to respond. "This wasn't something my mother had to deal with."

"But then you wouldn't be able to help Aunt Linda with her family and neighbors in Michigan."

Grandma gave her the side-eye. "Cheeky."

Janelle just grinned as the phone beeped a response.

Grandma typed out another message and hit send, then leaned back, looking pensive.

"You didn't know him, did you?" Janelle asked, gently.

"We met at the wedding, many years ago." She reached over and patted Janelle's arm. "I'm okay. Sometimes I forget how old I actually am. I don't feel like I'm seventy-four, but then someone from my generation dies, and I remember that I won't be around for much longer."

"Grandma!"

"Shush, it's a fact of life. But I want to be there for your special moments, and your cousins'. I want your mom and your aunt to be able to ask me how many stamps to send, or how much koden is appropriate, even if they argue with my opinion."

The very idea of her grandmother not being around made Janelle's heart ache. She loved the woman with her whole heart and knew that Grandma's loss would be devastating for the family. To not be able to send a photo of her and Naomi trying on outrageous dresses in Beverly Hills, as she'd done last week, or just to call and get the latest news on life in Hilo. She was suddenly happier than ever that Grandma had decided to come to Colorado for Rose's wedding.

Nell closed her eyes, her mind going back over their earlier conversation. As she'd said, she wasn't opposed to the idea of marriage, not at all. It was just getting harder and harder to imagine falling in love, wanting to tie herself, her future, to a man, but if she did, the idea that Grandma might not be there to see her married was too horrible to consider.

But here she was, on her way to a wedding. Seeing Rose and Ethan together had made her heart tingle in a way that her loins had steadfastly refused to do for ages. It made her incredibly happy to see them in love, and she had no doubt that theirs would last.

Janelle grinned as Naomi, meeting them at luggage claim, picked Grandma up in an enthusiastic hug.

"Grandma Yuki!"

Grandma's expression tried to maintain stoic, but she lost the battle and offered a wide smile. "I've missed you, too, Naomi. You didn't come to the island last year."

Naomi carefully lowered the older woman to the ground and stepped back. "I wanted to, but the timing just didn't work out. Next time."

"Good. Now, where are our bags? I'm anxious to meet this Ethan our Rose has decided on, make sure he's good enough for her."

Janelle waited until they were settled into the rental car, then leaned forward from the backseat. "So, how are the plans going? Is it crazy yet? Has Rose morphed into a bridezilla? I can't imagine it."

Naomi scoffed. "Of course she hasn't. She's being chill, though now that we're three days out, things have sped up a bit. For tonight, they're staying in for a quiet dinner while we get settled in. First thing tomorrow, it's on. There's a list of things for each of us."

"And tomorrow is the bachelorette party."

"Yes. Anna has ordered the stripper, the decorations you shipped are in a box in Ethan's office that he swears he hasn't opened, and one of us needs to pick up the desserts at the bakery while we're running around doing other things."

"Whew," she said quietly, seeing that Grandma's eyes had closed. "Sounds like everything is coming together."

"Yes. Cal and Jin, Rose's friends, had a nice dinner delivered from that restaurant we went to, Monarch?" She met Janelle's eyes in the rearview mirror.

Janelle nodded. She definitely remembered their night out at the fancy restaurant when they'd come out to meet Ethan.

"The guys gifted it to them so they could have one last quiet night in before all of the craziness happens. Ethan was going to insist on driving to pick you up tonight, because it was snowing and I'm not exactly experienced with that. But it finally stopped and I convinced him I could handle it and he and Rose should have their night."

"When do Jennifer and Brad get in? They're staying at the same B&B as us, right?"

"Yes, and so is Pablo. All of them get in tomorrow early afternoon. Jennifer and Brad will wait for Pablo, and they're sharing a car to get here, then Pablo and Brad will go away and leave the B&B to us for the bachelorette. We're taking over the whole place for the party since it's all just us."

Ah, Pablo, another friend from their old college group, one she hadn't seen in a few years. So much of the group had scattered after college, it wasn't unusual for them to only meet up at weddings. "I kind of wish Jennifer and Brad were bringing the baby so we could see her, but it's nice they'll be able to have this time away, too. Cammie's so cute, though it would have been weird to have a four-month-old at the bachelorette. And, wow, I haven't seen Pablo in years. I guess since Samantha Carney's wedding."

"Didn't he hit on you at her wedding?"

"Yes, but he was drunk."

"And you were there with…" Naomi squinted at the road ahead. "Derek. No, Darnel."

"Yep, Darnel. We'd been together six months, but only lasted three after that."

"He wanted to go to grad school in Nebraska."

"I told him I wasn't interested in Nebraska, but really it was more that I was tired of him moving from school to school rather than actually getting started in anything. I mean, if he'd had a realistic end goal, I could understand, but I really think it was just easier for him to keep being a student than to start paying his student loans."

"You were not wrong, my friend." Naomi glanced at her mirrors and moved lanes to pass a semi-truck. "Pablo seems to be coming single, and he was fairly attractive, as I recall. I want to say I've heard he's a veterinarian now?"

"I think I heard that, too. But, I mean, come on. He's a guy who hits on women who are in relationships."

"Fair point."

When they were an hour out, she called the pizza place in Wildlife Ridge, City Pizza, and told them when they expected to arrive at the B&B, prepaying with her credit card, including tip, and asking that the pizza arrive before they did. It had been a long travel day for Grandma, and she'd already told Rose that they would just head straight to the B&B and see her bright and early in the morning.

When she'd hung up, she sat back and watched the road race past for a few minutes. She'd been so excited, but also sad, when Rose had been the first of them to make a move, literally, by leaving Los Angeles and going to Colorado. Her plan had been to see if living there, in a lower-cost-of-living town than LA, would work, but really as a starting point to being able to live anywhere in the world. She dreamed of traveling while still supporting herself with her computer business. But she'd ended up falling in love with Wildlife Ridge, as much as she'd fallen for Ethan.

Still, she and Ethan were going to travel. Instead of a honeymoon, they were beginning a six-month stay in Spain. They'd bought a fixer-upper house in Wildlife Ridge that they were going to work on once they returned.

Janelle wanted to travel, but just for vacations. She wanted to find somewhere to settle down and be comfortable in her own place. Not that she wasn't comfortable in LA. Exactly. Sort of. She liked being able to go to museums once in a while, liked that there were restaurants galore, but really, she was kind of a homebody.

Those were once-in-a-while activities for her; there was no need to live in a big city like Los Angeles when you didn't love going out to the theater or a fancy restaurant or a concert three nights a week. And it definitely wasn't worth the traffic and crowds.

She'd taken a couple of vacations to small towns, hoping to find one that felt like home. So far, she had liked one, been annoyed by another, and had been indifferent to the third. The one she liked, in Eastern Washington, was a possibility, but she wasn't really sure it would hold up for the long term.

But, then again, she wasn't making a lifelong decision. If she moved once, she could do so again.

Naomi and Grandma were having a murmured conversation,

and Janelle realized she'd let her eyes close. She opened them to find that they were approaching Wildlife Ridge. Time to stop worrying about her future and start enjoying her time with friends.

One side of the highway was mountain, and the exit to Wildlife Ridge branched off the other side, nestling into a small valley that was backed by more mountains that she couldn't really see at night. It was more of a feeling of their looming presence and a lack of light.

But the town was lit and inviting. Main Street was where nearly all of the businesses in this town of less than twenty-five hundred people were located. There was only the one gas station first thing off the exit, one two-story strip mall and then several restaurants, including a couple of fast food joints, a Starbucks, and other miscellaneous shops.

She remembered a library, a Masonic Temple—she wasn't exactly sure she knew what that was—and a sheriff's station from her previous trip. The elementary school, and the junior and senior high school were just off Main Street, as were several small neighborhoods and a couple of apartment buildings.

Very quickly they passed the end of Elk Street, a one-way road that they wanted to be on. Only a few yards down, they were able to turn left onto the street. Elk Street made a giant cul-de-sac and came back around to Main. The space formed by the road was a giant lawn dotted with several trees, a little amphitheater, and Town Hall. This is where the wedding would be held.

When they had completed the loop and were most of the way back to Main Street, they turned right onto Glaring Road and made their way to the Columbine House B&B.

She'd made the arrangements for their stay and for the bachelorette party with Bob Bares, the owner, who was quick to come to the door to greet them and help them with their bags. She was very glad to see that the photos online hadn't done the beautiful house justice, and their rooms were excellent. Let the wedding weekend begin!

ABOUT THE AUTHOR

KB Alan lives the single life in Southern California. She acknowledges that she should probably turn off the computer and leave the house once in a while in order to find her own happily ever after, but for now she's content to delude herself with the theory that Mr. Right is bound to come knocking at her door through no real effort of her own. Please refrain from pointing out the many flaws in this system. Other comments, however, are happily received.

www.kbalan.com

To join KB's newsletter, visit www.kbalan.com/newsletter

facebook.com/kbalan

twitter.com/KB_Alan

instagram.com/authorkbalan

bookbub.com/authors/kb-alan

www.ingramcontent.com/pod-product-compliance
Lightning Source LLC
Chambersburg PA
CBHW071257190726
48292CB00007B/2578